Leon Garfield's stories are a rich and highly flavored stir-fry of eighteenth-century adventure. Under their wild story lines the books reveal an impressive knowledge of Victorian and Regency lowlife. Young readers are drawn in by the involved, mysterious plots, adults appreciate the black, sometimes outrageous humor. These are books for communal family reading, in the way that Dickens and Fielding were enjoyed by parents and children together in the nineteenth century. It is a fine thing that Leon Garfield's rip-roaring and funny tales should be brought back into circulation for a new generation of readers.      —*Joan Aiken*

Leon Garfield is unmatched for sheer, exciting storytelling; and, as well, for grand style and spirit. He has a perfect eye for character and a perfect ear for language. Whether suspenseful, droll, or deeply moving—or all this at the same time—his books are rich in color, bursting with vitality. He writes in the great tradition of English literature but his voice is uniquely his own. The reader simply can't stop reading him—and the rewards are magnificent.
      —*Lloyd Alexander*

I envy any reader discovering Leon Garfield. He's a wonderful storyteller!      —*Nancy Bond*

Leon Garfield was an inspired storyteller whose exuberant novels remind us of the unrivaled pleasures of reading. A brilliant stylist, Garfield was also a masterful plotter, whose novels are filled with mystery, secrets, surprises, and some of the most memorable characters since Dickens. Though chiefly set in the eighteenth century, his novels are timeless in their thematic treatment of good and evil and in their capacity to delight, stimulate, and satisfy. Leon Garfield's name belongs on everybody's shortlist of truly great writers for readers of all ages.                    —*Michael Cart*

Open a Leon Garfield novel and you'll be powerless until you've finished it. Nobody has ever equalled his glorious bloodcurdling mix of suspense, humor, and hypnotic storytelling.

—*Susan Cooper*

If James Bond were a twelve-year-old boy living in eighteenth-century England, his life of surprise and danger and self-discovery might have been recorded by Leon Garfield, just as he has brilliantly recorded the adventures of *Smith*, Bartholomew in *Black Jack*, and his other courageous and appealing young heroes.

—*Alison Lurie*

Some writers specialize in nifty plotting, learning from the movies how to pace a story like a foxhunt, a tiger chase. Some writers are noteworthy for the gleam and tension of their excellently wrought prose. Some writers relish building into their stories a dark and potent moral born, if we readers are lucky, of an uncompromising worldview. Few writers deliver all of the above. Leon Garfield does. He was head and shoulders above his contemporaries. He remains a talent to be remembered and a master to be emulated. Turn the pages fast, to gulp down the story; then start back at the beginning, to cherish the storytelling.          —*Gregory Maguire*

Born well into the twentieth century, Leon Garfield was the last great nineteenth-century author. Hooves rang on the paving stones of Dickens's London in Leon Garfield's mind. And he had the heart of a lamplighter, throwing and dispelling shadows. He handed the past to his readers because he never seemed to be looking back. Research? Undoubtedly, but something in his heart remembered.                                                          —*Richard Peck*

Leon Garfield's vivid descriptions and dialog transported me almost bodily into 18th-century England with characters as fully realized as the period and setting. Reissuing Leon Garfield's novels is a great gift to lovers of story of all ages.  —*Suzanne Fisher Staples*

Of all the talents that emerged in the field of British writing for children in the 1960s, that of Leon Garfield seems to me to be the richest and strangest. I am tempted to go on and say that his stories are the tallest, the deepest, the wildest, the most spine-chilling, the most humorous, the most energetic, the most extravagant, the most searching, the most everything.            —*John Rowe Townsend*

There has never been a writer to equal Garfield for ebullient, rip-roaring, gruesome, joyful, and witty evocation of the past, and for wonderful page-turning adventure stories. When is Garfield's past? You can't exactly place it—then as his tales unfold you understand that in his hands the past is a golden lantern, lighting up for us with penetrating tenderness and laughter and deep understanding the present and eternal nature of the human heart.

—*Jill Paton Walsh*

# THE STRANGE AFFAIR
# OF ADELAIDE HARRIS

L EON  G ARFIELD

# The Strange Affair
# of Adelaide Harris

F ARRAR  S TRAUS  G IROUX

N E W   Y O R K

Library of Congress Cataloging-in-Publication Data
Garfield, Leon.
    The strange affair of Adelaide Harris / Leon Garfield.—
Farrar, Straus and Giroux ed.
        p.   cm.
    Summary: An experiment to see if a wolf will adopt an abandoned baby turns into
a desperate situation for two schoolboys in early nineteenth-century England when
the child is recovered by well-meaning passersby.
    ISBN 0-374-37277-2
    [1. Humorous stories.   2. Great Britain—History—1789–1820—Fiction.]
I. Title.

PZ7.G17943 St 2001
[Fic]—dc21                                                                00-34131

*To Patrick Hardy*

# THE STRANGE AFFAIR
# OF ADELAIDE HARRIS

# I

A MUSTY, DUSTY, leathery smell of boys, books and ink. Words drone and a family of flies stagger through the heavy air as if in pursuit of them. But they turn out to be of Ancient History so the flies blunder moodily against the parlor window beyond which the June sun ripens tempting dinners at roadsides and down by the strong-smelling beach; day after day after day.

"Among the customs of ancient Sparta," says Mr. Brett at the twelve enormous, crumpled boys before him, and then goes on to tell of mothers bidding their sons come back *with* their shields or cold and dead *upon* them. He gazes at his twelve and reflects that Spartan mothers knew what they were about. He looks particularly hard at Bostock and Harris whom he hates and fears; day after day after day . . .

Thin, depressed, humane man—though with a touch of youth still remaining—Mr. Brett was employed to teach Classical Education at Dr. Bunnion's Academy in Brighton. There was something of a mystery about Mr. Brett; he was a well-spoken, gentlemanly sort of person, quite out of the usual run of schoolmasters. It was generally supposed that he'd fled from a well-to-do family in the north after committing some horrible crime and had found sanctuary in Dr. Bunnion's obscure school. This notion lent him a certain melancholy distinction in the eyes of the pupils and helped to explain why he never left the school for more than a few hours—even remaining through the holidays—and always tended to start and grow pale whenever there was a knock on the door.

From time to time, with the object of trapping Mr. Brett into betraying his crime, some ingenious pupil would ask seemingly innocent questions about parricides, fratricides and what were Mr. Brett's thoughts on poisonings (of which matters Ancient History was interestingly full), and then sit back and closely observe him for signs of guilty dismay.

Oddly enough, such questions did seem to disturb Mr. Brett in quite a striking way, and when some sly and brutish boy at the back, or the terrible Harris in the front, inquired how finely glass needed to be powdered before it might be used to commit murder, he would always falter and look alarmed . . . Then there'd fall an absolute silence on the class; the pupils would stare at Mr. Brett and Mr. Brett would stare at the pupils, and each would be struggling with his private thoughts of the other; and only God Almighty knew which was nearer the truth.

But now the day was almost done. Ten of the boys appeared to be asleep and Mr. Brett dropped his voice for he did not want to awaken them. Only Bostock and Harris still seemed to be interested in him. Side by side they sat in the front row and watched him attentively. Bostock was the larger of the two, but Harris was the deadlier. Though Bostock had caused more destruction and would, most likely, end on the gallows, Mr. Brett believed Harris to be his evil genius. Or would have believed it did not "genius" suggest a high intelligence—which Harris did not have. But there would be no more of them; so far as Mr. Brett was concerned, they were the end of their line. Harris had only a quantity of sisters and Bostock was a single child, so Mr. Brett thought that even his parents were appalled by what they'd done and would do no more.

Ten minutes of the lesson remained and Mr. Brett struggled on with the customs of ancient Sparta. A fat boy at the back was actually asleep with his mouth open. Mr. Brett had a childish desire to throw an ink pellet into it, but did nothing of the kind. The fat boy was a boarder at ninety pounds per annum and so worth three day pupils. Not for worlds would Mr. Brett have risked Dr. Bunnion's anger and, therefore, his situation. He was desperately anxious to remain. *Desperately* . . .

"Beg pardon, sir," said Harris, cupping an ear and leaning forward earnestly. "Can't quite hear you. Could I have that last item again?"

There was an unwholesome light in Harris's eyes. Uneasily Mr. Brett wondered what could have been the cause of it. He hoped it was a fever as he did not care to think of its being an idea.

"Little children," repeated Mr. Brett, as softly and tenderly as he could, "quite tiny infants exposed on the mountain side by their parents . . ."

Harris nodded shrewdly, and Mr. Brett caught himself wondering why the custom was ever abandoned. He would like to have lived in ancient Sparta—or, better, he would have liked Bostock and Harris to have lived there.

As these thoughts drifted into his mind, the bell rang and thunder from aloft proclaimed that Dr. Bunnion's Religious Instruction had finished for the day. Then all the little academy rocked and shook as Major Alexander's twelve rose from Arithmetic in the back parlor and all the six and thirty sons of merchants and gentle-folk tumbled fiercely out into the five o'clock sun. Even the fat boarder had gone—not to join his friends, for he had none—but to the kitchen, and Mr. Brett was left alone with his strange secret . . .

The unearthly light was still in Harris's eyes. Bostock noticed it and held his tongue. There was no point in interrupting his friend's thoughts; he would be told of them when Harris was ripe.

They lived in neighboring streets, about a mile and a half from the school, so there was time enough. As they walked, the sun streamed down and gave them immense shadows which fell like black phantoms among the half-built houses that littered their way—as if haunting them prematurely with the ghosts of tragedies to come. Their pace was slow; their manner winding, but sedate. There was no hurry. After some minutes of silence, Bostock stole a glance at his friend but it was plain that Harris's thoughts were still in the furnace, and at white heat. So Bostock scowled and punched an imaginary enemy. He was angry; he was often angry. It was part of his nature. Fits of anger came over him like waves of the sea till he longed to hiss and seethe and hurl stones like the sea itself. His father was a retired sea captain and he put it all down to that. Harris had once explained it to him—this notion of inherited passion—and Bostock had nodded fiercely, feeling at one with the elements. Harris's father, on the other hand, was a learned physician, so Harris was able to explain his own advanced manner of thinking in the same way.

They suited each other very well, did Bostock and Harris. Each had what the other lacked—and was always ready to part with it: Harris with his powerful mind and Bostock with his powerful limbs. In a way they represented the ancient idea of soul and body, but in a very pure state. Harris was as weak as a kitten and Bostock was as thick as a post. They were the greatest of friends and had the utmost respect for each other.

"I think he admires me, you know," said Harris abruptly.

"Who does?" asked Bostock, curious but not surprised.

"Mr. Brett."

"Oh," said Bostock, and waited. Whenever Harris opened his thoughts, the strange light in his eyes seemed to go out—like candles snuffed in an emptied room. But the light was still on, so Bostock knew there was more to come.

"Haven't you noticed how he looks at me and drops his voice like we was the only two in the room?"

The friends halted and Bostock stared down towards the wide, glittering sea where distant fishing vessels seemed like faint perforations on a blaze of silver. They had reached the corner of his street. Far away the clock of St. Nicholas's began to chime six and the setting sun, striking on the walls of the square flint houses, rosied the cobbles as if to show that even stone, when scrutinized by the eye of heaven, might have cause to blush.

Harris laid an inky finger on Bostock's torn, blue sleeve. Bostock stared and withdrew his eyes from the bright sea. "Old friend," murmured Harris, his large face seeming vague and luminous in Bostock's sun-dazzled eyes, "what do you say to this?"

Then he told Bostock what he had in mind. As he murmured on, now rapidly, now slowly, a wisp of cloud passed across the sun; the flushed houses changed their complexions and an unearthly gray pallor fell across the little golden street. There was a brief chill in the air—and Bostock shivered.

"Well?" said Harris softly.

Bostock gazed at him in terrified admiration. Harris wanted to expose an infant.

Among his numerous sisters, there was one of seven weeks old who was peculiarly suitable, and he was quite willing for Bostock to carry her up and expose her on the Downs. "It's a warm evening," he concluded with unusual humanity, "so I don't suppose she'll come to much harm. And anyway, my pa says it's wonderful what they can stand."

He stopped; the light had gone out in his eyes so Bostock knew he had finished. Bostock frowned. He knew Harris was not mad. There were good reasons behind Harris's scheme—very good reasons indeed. Only Bostock had not quite taken them in. A real tidal wave of anger at his own stupidity swept over him. He kicked a stone violently and watched it bounding down the street. Having no sisters of his own, he didn't presume to judge of Harris's generosity with his. The only living creature that Bostock had to share his meager thoughts and confidences with was a great brute of a ginger cat called Jupiter. Not for worlds would he have exposed Jupiter; but then he supposed cats were different. So Bostock, who would have trusted Harris with his life, helplessly nodded and hoped to understand everything in time.

Adelaide was the infant's name and Harris swore she was fed at six and then put down till she howled about four hours later. She wouldn't be missed.

Bostock felt himself being gently tugged towards the neighboring street where the Harris family lived a shade more elegantly than did the Bostocks. Already he could hear the faint shouts of the Harris girls and wondered, with a little pang, which was Mary's—for she had a thin, wild beauty that Bostock greatly admired.

"Quiet, Bosty—quiet as a mouse!"

Tiny Adelaide, fed and happy and dreaming her muslin dreams, snoozed in her crib while her giant sisters squabbled in the garden and the rest of the household obligingly forgot her. Of a sudden, she dreamed she was lifted into the air in a big fluffy cloud. She bubbled and chuckled and tightened her creased-up eyes against any interruption. She flew . . . she flew . . .

Bostock had got her partly under his coat. Leaving their loud boots in the street, the friends had entered the house, crept upstairs and abstracted the child. The fine weather had drawn everyone out of doors and only a kitchen maid had glimpsed them as they'd vanished through the front door. But she'd taken no particular notice. Master Harris and Master Bostock always came and went like ghosts—and were just about as welcome.

Once outside, the friends paused only to put on their boots before turning northward and hastening towards the Downs. This first, easy success of the scheme filled them with a trembling anticipation—though Bostock, heavily burdened, still did not know for what.

Already evening was coming on and the little town, lazy in the warm, buzzed only with the ever-busy flies. Silently the friends passed along the quiet, narrow streets; but always on the shady side. Ahead of them rose the great shoulders of the Downs where dark shadows were sweeping, like giants' hands lifting in abhorrence at the deep, inquiring brother and his patiently following friend. For, though Bostock was immensely strong, Adelaide was portly and her weight hampered his stride and kept him to the rear.

Tiny Adelaide dreamed she was in the branches of a tree and the wind was bouncing her up and down. She smiled into the musty darkness of Bostock's coat and her fat fingers found a waistcoat button . . .

"Harris!" Bostock's voice was sharp with alarm. "I—I think she's leaking or something. I'm all wet, Harris."

Harris hurried back and examined his sister. "I think she's peed, Bosty." For a moment the friends stared down at Adelaide in her cocoon of shawling—as if for the first time divining her to be vaguely as themselves, subject to the same pains, pleasures and natural laws. Then they observed the rapidly deepening sky and hastened on till the road dwindled away and became no more than a finger scratch of broken chalk through the stubby green.

On and on went Harris, across the uneven ground and skirting the chalky hollows that glared up abruptly, like the bleached sockets of half-buried giants' skulls. It was plain to the panting Bostock that Harris had one particular spot in mind. At last they reached it, and Bostock knew it well: a place of mystery, trysts and blackberries. It was a steep declivity, carpeted with close turf and bordered on three sides by thick, mysterious walls of bramble. This dense darkness was always full of strange rustlings and sudden cracklings as unseen denizens went about their sharp affairs.

"There," breathed Harris, pointing to the turf. "Lay her there."

Bostock hesitated, and Harris looked surprised. Then, and only then, did he understand that Bostock was totally ignorant of his purpose. At once a great warmth filled him as he realized the scope of his friend's trust. That Bostock should have come so far, and on so strange an errand just because he, Harris, had asked him, spoke volumes for the power of friendship. Harris blinked. Even though Bostock must have thought he was mad, he'd followed him without a word.

"Old friend," he whispered moistly. "You an' me's going to behold wonders."

Rapidly and eagerly he explained everything. Did Bostock recall the tale of the two Roman infants that were suckled by the she-wolf? Bostock frowned and nodded. Few things ever got into his mind, but when they did there was no getting them out again. They stayed there like the alien fixtures of another man's house—a source of passing wonder and bewilderment. He did not have the creative imagination that seizes on matters, apparently of little use and far apart, and instantly divines the link between them.

But Harris had. When Mr. Brett had mentioned the she-wolf, Harris's mind had leaped to the vixens that roamed the Downs; and when Mr. Brett had told of Spartan infants being exposed, Harris had thought at once of Adelaide. Then, putting all together in a sudden blaze, he'd hit on the inspired notion of seeing how native wildlife accepted a human baby in its midst. He had every hope, he whispered excitedly, of a vixen with full dugs coming to suckle Adelaide!

Bostock stared at Harris in awe. "Well?" said Harris; but Bostock was unable to speak, so Harris, mistaking his silence for doubt, said defensively, "Anyway, she's my sister and if she perishes it'll be me what'll have to bear her loss. Go on, Bosty—lay her down, old friend . . ."

Fat little Adelaide smiled and dreamed . . . dreamed she was being laid among buttercups and daisies on a cradling green . . .

Bostock and Harris crouched down to the windward in a patch of long grass through which only disconnected parts of them could be seen; and there, with bright, sharp eyes and pounding hearts, they awaited the arrival of the vixen with full dugs.

Harris never doubted for a moment that something of the kind would turn up and they'd witness an extraordinary phenomenon in nature; and Bostock never doubted Harris.

This is the most exciting moment of my whole life, thought Bostock; with difficulty. Harris is a real genius and he's my best friend. I'm so excited I could jump and shout and kick the grass. Something's going to happen. I don't know how to keep still. Who can I tell about it? I must . . . no, I mustn't. I wish I could think. Oh, I'm so horribly excited and Harris looks so calm. I wish I could stop thinking—someone might hear me . . .

Harris's thoughts, though no less turbulent, were of a more advanced nature and concerned the youngest person ever to read a learned paper before the Royal Society. Faintly, in his inner ear, he heard the bravos peal out like a storm of church bells on Judgment Sunday, and he bowed his head to hide his happy tears . . .

Suddenly the two friends grew still in mind and body. A sound had petrified them. A faint but unmistakable panting and snuffling and crackling of bramble. Then there was a crunching of dry twigs. Harris's face, briefly blossoming in the long grass, was ashy with expectation.

Little Adelaide, deep in her blind sleep, chuckled and dreamed she was about to be fed again . . .

---

It was coming, it was coming! The vixen—the vixen with full dugs!

# 2

YOUNG, PRETTY and in yellow muslin, Tizzy Alexander, daughter of the fiery Major who taught Arithmetic, was in a condition of terrified excitement. Her heart was thumping half out of her bodice and she kept clutching at her scarf to hide it. She must have been mad to have put herself in Ralph Bunnion's way but wild curiosity had at last overpowered her. Ralph Bunnion—cricketer, horseman and hero of the school. What was he like—this terrible, handsome, heartless breaker of hearts? Tall, fashionable and, so far as could be judged from the ends of them, clean-limbed.

The use of this last expression had given her a brief feeling of maturity but it had gone when she'd stolen glance after glance at Dr. Bunnion's dashing and notorious son. It was said he'd once fought a duel—and everyone knew he drank prodigious quantities of claret at the Old Ship Inn with three young men almost as famous as himself.

Oh, Tizzy, why ain't you back in the school, safe with your ma and pa? She shook her head. In her heart of hearts she knew she'd always have regretted it. She knew that, if she missed this chance, she'd have dreamed and wondered all her life long what it would have been like to have been swept off her feet by a Ralph Bunnion. Only once in a lifetime did such an adventure befall a young girl.

With a start she felt his hand on her arm and she realized they'd walked all the way from the school to the beginning of the Downs. All her instincts bade her fly back home; but she could not. The sun was dropping down and warning shadows were pooling in the rough, tufted ground like treacherous black pits. Tizzy—Tizzy! When will it begin? Oh, Tizzy, what a little fool you are! Thus her fears and hopes raced hand in hand.

He was talking to her, had been for some time, but she'd been too engrossed in her own confused sensations to know what he'd been saying. All she'd noticed was that, as he laughed, his teeth flashed like bayonets.

Lord! He was handsome! He wore a mouse-colored coat with smart tails and a waistcoat embroidered with a design of love-lies-bleeding.

"D'you know," he said, laughing gently, "the last time I walked this way was with poor Maggie Hemp?"

"Oh dear," said Tizzy. "I saw her only yesterday in Bartholomew's. I didn't know aught was amiss—"

"Then—then she's not—not drowned?"

"Oh no—"

"Thank God!" breathed Ralph fervently. "I say thank God for that!"

"I never knew," began Tizzy, when Ralph shook his head as if the subject was painful to him. But in a little while he overcame his distress and admitted to Tizzy that Maggie Hemp had threatened to throw herself off Black Rock and into the pounding sea.

"Why?" asked Tizzy. Ralph glanced at her a shade coldly.

"Who knows the secrets of a woman's heart?" he wondered aloud; and then went on to explain that Lizzy Cooper had come between them. He believed it possible that Maggie's affections were more deeply engaged than he'd supposed, and it distressed him very much. He wished such things wouldn't keep happening to him for he was, by nature, retiring and shy. "As I was saying to Dolly Packer, only last night at the Assembly Rooms, she shouldn't set her heart on me . . ."

"And poor—poor Miss Cooper?" whispered Tizzy, in deeper waters than ever she'd supposed. Ralph sighed, shrugged his broad shoulders and tightened his grip on her arm. Tizzy moaned inwardly and saw herself poised on some cruel eminence with the wind blowing her pretty ringlets, crying, "Ralph!" as she leaped to a popular oblivion.

"You women!" said the hapless Ralph, laughing ruefully. "We men don't stand a chance!"

Imperceptibly their pace had quickened. Ahead lay a dangerously romantic-looking hedge of brambles that crowned a scooped-out bed of turf. Such mysterious trysting places had often figured in Tizzy's dreams—such lovers' couches of green with leafy curtains to shut out the eyes of the world.

Her heart fluttered and she looked, half yearningly, back along the way they'd come. With a pang she saw the humdrum little town far below. It looked for all the world as though it had slipped down the green hillsides and come to rest at the edge of the wide swallowing sea for the greater convenience of Ralph Bunnion's unhappy loves.

"You snare us and trap us with your charms," said Ralph, laughing bitterly now. Tizzy waited, nervously hopeful of discovering which of her charms was proving the deadliest. But it was not to be. Instead she learned to her dismay that Ralph was as clay in women's hands. Somehow or another they always seemed to be attracted to him. He didn't know why, but wondered if there might be some sort of shining about him.

He paused and eyed her with an air of weary expectancy. Tizzy blushed and looked hurriedly down at her black shoes popping in and out of her daffodil gown and carrying her onward to her fate. Ralph laughed, frowning this time, and admitted that his mysterious attractiveness was really quite unwelcome. There were times, even, when he dreaded it and envied his friends who might go anywhere without so much as a single admiring look.

Could she, Tizzy, understand how wretched it was that every time he stood up to dance at the Old Ship Assembly Rooms everyone fell back to watch? Yes, he *was* a fine dancer; but then so were many others. Yes, he *was* a brilliant cricketer; but so were several others. Yes, he *was* a remarkable horseman; but there were others almost as good. So what was it?

He felt so—so foolish about it all. More often than not he longed to be at home with a good book; but it was never to be. What *was* it about him, he demanded of Tizzy. Was he—here he laughed incredulously—was he really so outrageously handsome?

"No—no!" breathed Tizzy, confused and grateful to have been brought into the conversation.

Ralph glared at her. He'd underplayed his hand and been too modest. It was a weakness of his. He kicked a lump of chalk, laughed fiercely and said, "Dolly Packer once said I was like a Greek statue . . ."

Tizzy looked up. The dark and secret hedge of bramble was almost upon them. She thought of the soft green bed it screened but, to her surprise, she felt nothing of the terrified expectancy with which she'd set out. Perhaps she was being swept off her feet without knowing it? She sighed. Was life always such a disappointment? Was she never to learn that her eyes were like mysterious twilit pools and her lips a pair of kissing cherries? Was she never to share those high, sweet passions with which the lovers of old led each other up the mountains of bliss?

"Dolly said my profile was extraordinarily Greek . . ." He presented this aspect of himself for Tizzy's admiration. Unluckily Tizzy was still brooding on life's disappointments, and her expression was touched with something very like boredom. Fatally offended, the handsome Ralph felt one of his rages coming on. As through a veil of red, he saw Tizzy just ahead of him. She was picking her way round the bramble hedge to the very edge of the soft, grassy couch. Angry, lustful thoughts inflamed him. He would teach her what it meant to be out with Ralph Bunnion. There was a terrible look in his eyes, and with a savage laugh he launched himself at Tizzy, meaning to seize her and bear her to the amorous ground.

At the selfsame moment Tizzy saw, of all amazing things, a tiny human baby, lying all alone, asleep in the grass. She cried out, "Lord save us! A baby!" and rushed to gather it up.

Thus it happened that, with nothing in the way to halt him, Ralph Bunnion, still laughing savagely, flew a goodish way across the declivity before coming down and striking the ground with his face. He gave a sharp, loud cry of pain, but Tizzy urgently begged him to be quiet as the baby was sleeping.

Tiny Adelaide dreamed of deliciously frightening storms and thunder; then she chuckled as she fancied herself to be borne up and floating in a sea of milk . . . gently, gently towards some crisp, entrancing shore . . .

"The shame of it," murmured Tizzy Alexander, walking with the greatest care and tenderness as she bore her precious burden. "To leave such a sweet thing to die! Lord, what's the world coming to? What can have come over the mother to part with her darling soft morsel?"

Ralph Bunnion did not answer. He was not interested. He followed after Tizzy with a handkerchief pressed to his face. He had suffered severe scratches and bruises and his nose would not stop bleeding. He feared it might have been put out of shape. He had heard of such things. He was consumed with hatred for Tizzy and the infant in her arms.

"What should we do with it, Mr. Bunnion? We can't just let it go on the parish. Perhaps it could go to the Foundlings? But wouldn't that be a shame? It's such a darling. And—and finding it so. I get a queer shivering that we were *meant* to come on it as we did . . . as if it's something special like Moses in the bulrushes or—or Perseus in his ark. Maybe it's going to grow up into a saint or a hero or something. Oh, Mr. Bunnion! D'you think we could keep it? It wouldn't be no trouble. We could give it every love and care and Pa could teach it Arithmetic . . ."

Thus Tizzy prattled on, her motherly feelings shining in her flushed and sweet young face. All the benefits of love, affection and learning could be lavished on the mysterious infant. Nothing would be denied it . . .

A little way behind her stalked Ralph Bunnion, his face—and particularly his nose—blazing with pain. Dimly he thought of revenging himself on Tizzy, but was too upset to determine on how. Vague images of dark figures overwhelming her filled his dazed brain. He shifted the handkerchief and discovered that the blood still flowed. He hoped he'd not lost too much; and above all he hoped he'd not stained his father's best cravat which he happened to be wearing. More and more passionate grew his hatred of Tizzy Alexander . . .

A little way behind him, taking skillful advantage of every bush and sheltering hollow, crept Bostock and Harris, awed beyond measure by the fate that had overtaken Adelaide. Though Bostock had been deeply moved by Miss Alexander's tenderness and the wonderful prospect she'd held out for the infant, he knew it wouldn't be right to let Adelaide go. He peered towards Harris whose face was of a terrible whiteness. So Bostock held his peace till he should be told what to do. Harris would think of something. Harris was nobody's fool . . .

Thus thought Bostock as he followed Harris who followed the famous Ralph Bunnion who followed Tizzy Alexander and Adelaide in strange procession towards Dr. Bunnion's Academy . . .

# 3

MR. BRETT, DESPISED even by the cook for never flaring up like the lively Major Alexander and bearing every humiliation as if his very life depended on staying at Dr. Bunnion's, sat at dinner next to the fat boarder whose name was Sorley. Though there were two other boarders at ninety pounds per annum each, Sorley came first in the headmaster's estimation. He was the son of a baronet at Cuckfield and Dr. Bunnion had hopes concerning a sister of Sorley's and his own son, the ever-popular Ralph. But he was a sensible man and kept these hopes to himself, and only assisted them by throwing in Sorley's way any little advantage or courtesy that might be reported back to Cuckfield. Naturally he looked to his staff to do the same. In his heart of hearts he considered his ambitions not unreasonable; Sorley, in common with the rest of the school, looked up to the handsome Ralph as to a prince . . . and surely must have talked of him at home.

"Here, boy," said Major Alexander, leaning across the table and thoughtfully helping Sorley to more mutton pie. "We must look after you, eh?"

Mr. Brett, who was sitting next to Sorley and so might have performed the same action more easily, bit his lip. As usual, his thoughts had been elsewhere so Major Alexander benefited by a smile from Dr. Bunnion while he received a look of contempt from the doctor's stately wife. Mr. Brett lowered his eyes and wondered if life was worth living.

It was then that there came an agitated knocking on the door. It was a rapid and urgent sound; the door seemed to tremble and before Dr. Bunnion could speak, it burst open.

At the same moment two faces of supernatural terror appeared at the window, then vanished like spectral dreams, blown by the wind. No one in the room had seen them nor felt the stare of their wild eyes. They had made no sound nor even misted the glass with their breath. They had not dared to breathe.

But in that instant Bostock and Harris had seen Harris's infant sister in Miss Alexander's arms being presented at Dr. Bunnion's dining table like an extra course. Ralph Bunnion was not with her; she and Adelaide stood alone before the astonished company. Harris thought madly of tapping on the window and coming out with: "Please can we have our baby back?" but natural dread of the unlucky affair being told to his father killed the idea stone dead. If there was any hope at all—for him, for Bostock and for little Adelaide—it rested in the god of boys and infants, to whom Harris unscientifically prayed.

"And what, miss, were you doing on the Downs with Mr. Bunnion?" Major Alexander, being an ex-officer of Engineers, had a fiery and explosive sense of honor which he was inclined to lay like mines under friends and enemies alike. Generally no great harm was done owing to the Major's natural deviousness. He tunneled too far and explosives were apt to go off at too great a distance from the events that had provoked them; thus his fury often seemed more the result of brooding on some unworthy trifle than the instant anger of an honorable man.

But this time he'd exploded his mine with military speed and success. Instantly Adelaide was forgotten and Tizzy's tender pleadings on the baby's behalf were blown to smithereens.

"Well, miss?"

The Major was standing. He was a short, square, formidable man with flashing eyes. Tizzy went very red and Mrs. Alexander, a German lady, shrugged her shoulders and muttered something in her native tongue.

"I—I—" stammered Tizzy, guiltily recalling the dreams with which she'd set out. "That is, Pa, we was walking—"

"Indeed, miss?" said Major Alexander in a low, shaking voice. "Alone—with Mr. Bunnion? I rather fancy you are lying to me. I rather fancy he has—compromised you, miss. As I see it, this is a matter of *honor*."

The word honor was delivered like a sword thrust, and Ralph's father felt a warning stab at his heart.

"My dear Major," began Dr. Bunnion, hurriedly attempting to calm his touchy Arithmetic master, "even allowing for your—um—impulsive—er—nature, there's really no need . . . a trifle, really—"

"A *trifle?*" The Major clenched his fists. "My daughter's honor a trifle?"

"My dear sir—I didn't mean that. You misunderstand me. I would never dream of implying such a thing." The headmaster spoke with almost trembling sincerity. He was a man who valued discretion above all and the conversation was becoming painful to him. "Miss Alexander herself has said they were just walking. She brings no charge—no charge at all. And I assure you, sir, my boy Ralph is the soul of gentility. To my knowledge he has never harmed a fly. I beg of you, sir, most earnestly, to—to control yourself, if you'll forgive the expression. Of course I respect your feelings, but I am certain, quite, quite certain that you are mistaken . . . indeed, damned nonsense!"

This last remark had been quite unintentional, but the headmaster was deeply agitated. He kept glancing at Sorley as if wondering how much of the scene would be reported to Cuckfield.

"Fetch my son," said Mrs. Bunnion coldly, "and put an end to this at once. Whatever that girl" (here she glanced contemptuously at the scarlet Tizzy) "may say, my son will tell the truth. Rest assured of that, Major Alexander. Mr. Bunnion will tell you your odious suspicions are as absurd as they are insulting."

Dr. Bunnion, while wishing his wife had not spoken out so plainly, none the less agreed that Ralph ought to defend himself and put an end to the wretched scene. So he was sent for . . .

Unluckily, Ralph—after congratulating himself on having reached his room without being seen—had not yet restored his dapper appearance. Such was the unexpectedness of the summons that he'd scarcely time to remove his damaged coat and his father's cravat before presenting himself to the company in his fatal waistcoat with its design of love-lies-bleeding, and with a similar design, executed in blood, on his brow and nose.

Mr. Brett's lips twisted in a bitter smile.

"I see my child defended herself," said Major Alexander harshly. There could be no reasonable doubt that the young man's injuries had been inflicted by the desperate and outraged nails of the Major's daughter. "I rather fancy I am entitled to—satisfaction."

At once there was a terrible silence in the room. The scene which had, at the very worst, been disagreeable and awkward, took on an edge of steel. Dr. Bunnion stared aghast at his son and the smoldering Major and seemed to see phantom bullet holes in their breasts—and all his dreams and ambitions sinking in a sea of scandalous blood.

"My God," he whispered. "You—you cannot mean a—a duel?"

Now Major Alexander had not meant a duel. Nothing had been further from his thoughts. He had meant to say "compensation" but thought it sounded too mercenary and so had said "satisfaction" instead. He was as shocked as anybody by the turn affairs had taken; he frowned uneasily at the athletic Ralph who did not look the sort of opponent to be trifled with. There was an unpleasantly fearless look about him that the Major could not help disliking; and in a moment his worst fears were realized. Ralph, conscious of the adoring eyes of the three boarders fixed upon him, drew himself up and said coolly, "I am at your service, sir."

"For God's sake!" cried Dr. Bunnion. "Can we not talk this over?"

"Yes!" said Major Alexander eagerly.

"Pa! Mr. Bunnion!" moaned Tizzy in terror—when the infant in her arms, disregarded till that moment, woke up and began to scream and scream.

Tiny Adelaide had opened her eyes. Huge strange faces filled her sky and whirled like furious suns as far as she could see. She struggled to put up her fat little hands to push them away . . .

"Get rid of that baby!" shouted Dr. Bunnion. "Get it out of here!" The wailing of Adelaide, filling the little Academy with its despair, had set up a multitude of echoes in the headmaster's head till he could no longer think. Tizzy pleaded and begged for the infant to go to the Foundlings—as it no longer seemed probable that she'd be allowed to keep it—but Dr. Bunnion, who had a mania for discretion, was all for quietness; so, still shouting above the infantine uproar, he insisted it be taken and left in the church porch for the vicar to deal with. Tizzy protested that it was inhuman and that they were all beasts and brutes who thought only of themselves and that it was shameful to turn away one so young and helpless.

"Hold your tongue, miss!" snarled the Major. "It's you who are inhuman to think of a damned baby when your pa is prepared to sacrifice his life to clear your honor!"

"I'll take it," offered Ralph. "I'll ride like the wind, sir . . ."

"You're savages, savages!" wept Tizzy, clinging to the baby

which seemed to her the only real and warm thing in the whole de-mented room. They were a very sweet and touching sight—the girl and the crying baby—but it was only Mr. Brett who pitied them as they were parted, and Adelaide was given up to the eager, handsome Ralph.

Like brooding spirits Bostock and Harris moved from under the window and followed the wailing that had come out into the air.

"We'll get her back from the church," breathed Harris, and thanked the god of boys and infants for so aptly answering his prayers.

Pressed against the wall they waited for Ralph Bunnion to emerge from the little yard, high on the school horse. There was something wild and noble about the headmaster's son as he leaned forward against the evening sky with one hand on the reins and the other about the crying child. There was something of an ancient story and a deathless ride as he clattered away in a cloud of fright-ened sobs.

Bostock and Harris followed after, at first cautiously, then faster and faster till their boots seemed winged. On and on they sped, leaving behind them the little Academy which was now trembling in the grip of its own, quite separate calamity.

Presently the sound of the infant's wailing stopped as the mo-tion of the horse rocked it back into sleep; then the sound of the horse itself died away and all that could be heard was the groaning breath and stumbling footfalls of the two pursuers as they mounted the hill towards St. Nicholas's.

"There he goes!" panted Harris as he looked up and saw the

dark shape of the great horseman bending low over his burden; but it was only for a moment—the strange pair vanished almost instantly into the stony bulk of the aged, sometime haunted church.

"Hurry—hurry!" urged Harris. He was horribly afraid they'd be too late and Adelaide would be snatched inside before they could recover her. At last they reached the shadow of the church. There was no sign of horse or rider. Ralph Bunnion, master horseman, had been true to his word; he had come and gone like the invisible wind.

White of face and silent of step, the friends crept through the churchyard. Suddenly a movement disturbed them. They melted amid the monuments and with fearful eyes observed a solitary mourner—a gypsyish widow—rustle tragically away. Once or twice she stopped to look back, then she vanished like a ghost.

"Look, Bosty!" whispered Harris, pointing to the dark porch. "She's still there!"

Bostock looked; a quiet bundle lay upon the step. "Thank the Lord!" he breathed, and sped like an arrow to gather it up and follow his friend down the hill.

With hearts almost bursting but with spirits high, they ran and ran till they reached the fateful corner of the street where the adventure had begun. As they did so, the clock of St. Nicholas's chimed a quarter to ten. Fifteen minutes remained for the friends to return Adelaide to her crib and call it a day.

"Best give her to me, now, Bosty," said Harris when they were but yards from his home. Thankfully Bostock handed over the still quiet bundle to its lawful flesh and blood.

"You know, Bosty," murmured Harris with unusual tenderness and affection, "I'm glad we got her back. I mean, after all, she *is* my sister . . ."

He unwound a corner of the shawl to see how his sister did. He trembled; he moaned; he shook so violently that the infant almost fell and Bostock put out a hand to save it.

The tiny face, sleeping in its wrappings, was of a crumpled brownish color, with scanty hair as black as sin. Even in the fragile light of the broken moon, there was no doubt. It was not Adelaide. They had got the wrong baby.

Far, far away, tiny Adelaide opened her eyes and gurgled with joy. Mistily she saw a golden bird hovering over her head. She reached up to pluck a feather from its wings . . . pretty bird . . .

She lay under the lectern, not in St. Nicholas's but in the church at Preston beyond, where Ralph Bunnion had left her. The master horseman, up on the school horse—which he was not allowed to ride as often as he would have liked—had been unable to resist the temptation of galloping further afield than to St. Nicholas's and back. So he had gone on to Preston . . .

"Are you sure, Harris?" whispered Bostock, dimly sensing the enormous disaster and struggling to deny it. For answer Harris glared at his friend with terrible eyes set in a face beside which the pallid moon was rosy. Of course he was sure. What was to be done? Piteously Bostock gazed at Harris for instructions. Such was his admiration and the size of his heart that he would have done anything for his friend. He would have plucked the cock from the church steeple; he would have brought him an alderman's ring or the mayor's chain if only Harris would speak and command.

But what could Harris do or say? Even had he ten Bostocks at his command, there was too little time. Minutes alone remained to fill the empty cot in the Harris nursery and dispose of the beetle-browed babe in his trembling arms.

Then panic inspired him. "Bosty," he whispered. "We'll have to put it in Adelaide's place."

Bostock stared at him in veneration; then a doubt soiled its edges. "But—but won't they notice?"

Harris shrugged his shoulders. Having decided on his course, a feeling of deathly calm had overcome him. "What else can we do, Bosty? Answer me that. What else *is* there?"

The two friends gazed at each other over the head of the sleeping baby; the one resolved, the other still hesitant. Then Bostock knew, in his heart of hearts, that Harris's was the only way. "You're a genius, Harris."

Palely, Harris nodded and, returning the infant to Bostock, beckoned him on. As they neared the unsuspecting house, once more they removed their boots and flitted on with phantom stealth. A moment later, the small street was deserted and the riding moon stared down on the empty boots which lay like mysterious vessels on the shore of adventure . . .

# 4

MR. BRETT LAY IN his bed in the awkward attic where even the moon came in contemptuously. It laid a silver finger across the humble blanket as if wondering whether it was a man or a mouse that lay so quietly beneath. Wake up, wake up, James Brett, it seemed to say, or be buried forever in this dull spot!

But Mr. Brett did not seem to heed the moon's warning; instead he brooded on the evening's alarm. Though he was a peace-loving man, opposed to all violence save in the Ancient World where heroes battered each other's immortal brains out till a turn of the page resurrected them, the prospect of a duel between Major Alexander and Ralph Bunnion excited him enormously. Like the worried father, he, too, dreamed of phantom bullet holes in proud breasts, but, unlike the father, he cared not in which. Both the adversaries had cast their shadows across his secret life, and he detested them equally.

Mr. Brett's secret led him down strange paths and gave him bloody thoughts. But they were only thoughts, for his secret itself was of the softest kind. He was in love! Helplessly, frantically, wildly and, above all, hopelessly, he was in love with Tizzy Alexander. The very sound of her footfall made him tremble and the sight of her face obstructed his heart. He no longer knew whether he'd come to this state little by little or whether, in the winking of an unguarded eye, he'd fallen into the midst of the sea of desire in which he now floundered.

But, however it had begun, it was now an exquisite torment and a marvelous misery. He dared not breathe a word of his passion; he was violently terrified she would laugh at him and so extinguish the forlorn hope he still nursed. So he quaked and turned pale to every knock on the door and endured all the miseries of life in Dr. Bunnion's school. He became a walking knot of complicated emotions that daily tightened about his heart and caused him to snarl and snap at the one being he loved to distraction.

He sighed and gave a tortured smile. Whether or not the duel and the possible deaths of the Major and the headmaster's lecherous son would improve his situation was doubtful; but he didn't see that it could do any harm.

Suddenly there came a knock on the door. The smile left his face and a look of uncertainty and dread replaced it. He sat up. "Who's there?"

The door opened and Tizzy Alexander in her shift with a netted black shawl about her shoulders came in. Amazed and intoxicated he stared at her, and, before he could utter a word, she raised her finger to her lips and gently closed the door. "You must help me," she whispered.

"For pity's sake," he breathed, "go back to your room! What— what would your mother say?" His heart thundered as passion and propriety fought a battle in his breast beside which the fury of Hector and Achilles was as but a tiff between children.

"Ma sent me," said Tizzy, with a worried smile that was intended to reassure Mr. Brett, but did not.

"In heaven's name, why?" Such was Mr. Brett's terror and excitement that his voice took on an edge he deeply regretted.

"She said you was the only one in the house with any sense," said Tizzy nervously. "She said you was the only one who could stop them fighting . . ." Then Tizzy, quite overcome by the horrible circumstance, sat down on the edge of the bed and began to cry. "They'll kill each other," she wept, "and I'll be to blame for it."

"Isn't that what young women dream of?" muttered Mr. Brett bitterly. "To have men fight to the death on their account?"

Once again he regretted his words. That Tizzy had come to him filled his heart with joy; but that she'd come only to beg his help in preventing the very thing he half hoped would happen was a deep humiliation. None the less the sight of her weeping in the moonlight moved him almost unbearably and it was as much as he could do to stop himself folding her in his aching arms. The coldness of his words had been more to cool his own ardor than to reproach Tizzy. But she, who knew nothing of this, raised her eyes and looked at him in utter misery.

"I thought . . . I thought you would understand."

"Oh, but I do understand!" said Mr. Brett rapidly, and went on to lash himself still more with his own cruel tongue. "I understand very well, Miss Alexander! I understand you're frightened out of your wits for what your silly, flirting little heart has brought about! I understand that you don't know where to turn for escape! I understand that you're willing to do anything—even to come to the wretched, despised Mr. Brett in the attic to implore him to save your lover from the wrath of your father—"

"He's never my lover!" sobbed Tizzy furiously. "I hate him! I hate you! I hate everybody!" She stood up and wore the moonbeam from the window like a sash. "I wish I was dead! I—I'll drown myself like—like—"

"Ophelia?" offered Mr. Brett savagely.

"No," said Tizzy with sudden dignity. "Like Maggie Hemp."

With that she swept from the room leaving the moonbeam empty and Mr. Brett in an agitated torment of misery, wondering why he was always his own worst enemy. You fool, you fool! he groaned to himself, you've killed your only hope! Why did you do it? Why do you always do it?

Then, as the storm subsided, the answer came to him cold and clear. It was because he despised himself more than anyone else he knew. Not even in his dreams of ancient grandeur could he ever aspire to anything. The armor of Achilles would have crushed him and the very sight of Hector's nodding plume would have sent him shrieking from the field. He was a pygmy, a dwarf beside whom even that lout Ralph Bunnion stood up for a man.

Tizzy and Mr. Brett were not the only ones denied the ease of sleep. Dr. Bunnion was restless, too. He had dozed off but his dreams had been of so alarming a nature and a sharp creaking of floorboards or joists had so fitted in with the dread of a leveled pistol that he'd woken with a faint cry and had not dared close his eyes since.

The thought of the duel fell like the hand of death across his imaginings. Although in private the fiery Major had offered to withdraw his challenge, his conditions had been as hateful to Dr. Bunnion as the prospect of the fight itself. To wipe out the stain on his family honor, the Major had had the impudence to propose a marriage between the handsome Ralph and his own child, the penniless, wretched Tizzy. He had said it and stood back with almost a smile. It was plain he'd not budge an inch.

Dr. Bunnion scowled into the darkness of his bed and contemplated informing a magistrate of the duel and so having the Major jailed for two years. This at least would save Ralph, and if news of the affair could be prevented from reaching Cuckfield, there would still be hope for the baronet's daughter. But, on the other hand, it would deprive the school of its Arithmetic master and of Mrs. Alexander who taught German.

He sighed and gently eased his huge body out of the bed where Mrs. Bunnion slept like a stately ship, rising and falling at anchor.

He paced the room, then, shaking his head, quietly opened the door and went out in search of a solution to his problems.

He passed along the passage until it joined another where his candle illuminated both ways as if to give him a choice of direction. He paused, frowned, then seemed to make up his mind. Quietly he moved down one passage while his shadow seemed to go down another.

There were a great many such passages in the upper part of the Academy, linking, dividing and turning sharply away. Sometimes there were stairs between—not flights but single steps that seemed like spies from lost battalions, lying in wait and wondering where the rest had gone. All this was in consequence of Dr. Bunnion's desire to expand his premises. He had knocked through and thrown out in so many directions that the house itself had come to resemble a pupil, endlessly outgrowing its suit of bricks. Had there been such a word, Dr. Bunnion would have called himself an educationalist; he got his living from education and was dedicated to expanding that living by expanding his capacity to educate.

Such then was the hapless complication of corridors that the prowling headmaster did not meet with Tizzy who, having left Mr. Brett, was drifting round strange corners like a melancholy ghost. Her agitated tears still flowed and, having more pride than sense, she would not return to her room from which her mother could have heard her sobs of distress.

"Come in!" breathed Mr. Brett. There had come a second knock on his door. His heart had leaped; she had forgiven him! Now for certain he would tell her of his love. His voice trembled with hope . . .

The door opened and Major Alexander slipped in with the air of looking for somewhere to lay a mine.

An unreasonable anger seized Mr. Brett, and it was so apparent that the Major felt obliged to apologize for having disturbed him. Mr. Brett neither accepted nor rejected the apology, but seemed to leave it in the air like an invisible third party between them.

"Brett, my dear fellow," murmured the Major, shifting restlessly round the little room. "I've come to beg a favor." He had reached the window and frowned out on to the night world; then, with sharp, sidelong glances at the foot of the bed, went on: "I know you and I haven't always seen eye to eye but I've always understood our differences were honorable." Here he looked inquisitively at the top of Mr. Brett's head. "We've differed on principle alone—but I've always felt our natures, underneath it all, to be sincerely friendly."

Mr. Brett, who had felt no such thing, mumbled feebly into his blanket and the Major nodded. "Truth of the matter is, Brett, I need your help. This—this shocking affair . . . if it comes to anything (and we all pray it won't), well, the upshot is, I'd like you to act as me second."

"*What?*"

"Second, my dear fellow. Arrange all the details: weapons et cetera . . . time and place . . . surgeon . . ."

Mr. Brett sat bolt upright. Weapons? Surgeon? He knew nothing about such matters. He knew nothing about dueling.

"You ain't engaged for the—um—other side?" asked the Major, whose first instinct was to assume everyone was as devious as himself. "If so I'd rather you came out with it openly, Brett. You know me—man of honor—can't abide subterfuge—all in the open—no excuses—"

Mr. Brett stared at him and wondered that such a father could have produced such a daughter. Then the unworthy thought struck him that such a father had not produced such a daughter and that Mrs. Alexander had been swept off her feet by some unlawful broom . . . He smiled, and the Major, mistaking his expression, darted up to him, shook him warmly by the hand and exclaimed, "Thank you, Brett. From the bottom of my heart. Knew I could count on you. Pays to open one's heart . . . always . . ."

With a last affectionate squeeze of Mr. Brett's helpless hand and a last reference to his heart's bottom, he vanished from the room, leaving behind a faint smell of brandy and sweat as if in token of having briefly opened that secret place in his breast. Once outside, the Major paused for a moment, cocked his head towards the door, then departed, wearing that curious smile that nature has drawn on the jaws of snakes and crocodiles.

He moved swiftly and silently, and even as the pale skirt of his nightgown whisked round a corner a flickering light and accompanying shadow approached from the opposite direction.

"For God's sake, what now?" groaned Mr. Brett, and his third visitor came in.

Dr. Bunnion, gowned and candled, seemed to fill the tiny room like some immense spirit on a dreadful errand to guilty beds. This severity of aspect was, however, the work of nature and could not be helped. Within was a very discreet and hopeful gentleman, even timid at times.

"Jack," he murmured. "I may call you Jack, I take it?"

Mr. Brett nodded. His name was James, but it did not seem to signify.

"This unhappy affair, you know. Of course, one cannot blame

Alexander. These military men and their honor . . . where would we be without them? I blame the girl, I'm afraid. But still, what's done is done and we must all face the consequences and look to the future . . ."

He drifted on in this way for some minutes while his candle tilted and shed its wax on Mr. Brett's folded breeches. Angrily Mr. Brett watched and, each time the headmaster paused for breath, attempted to draw attention to the circumstance.

"So, Jack, you understand why I'd rather it was you than any of Ralph's wild friends. So long as there's a chance of reconciliation, it's important to have someone of good sense acting as his second." The headmaster smiled painfully. "Thank you for bearing with me, Jack. And above all, thank you for standing by me—standing by the school, I should say—in this time of trial. But then I knew I could count on you, Jack . . ." He shifted his candle so that a final little cataract of wax fell on the folded breeches before wishing Mr. Brett a heartfelt good night. A moment later he popped his large head back into the room and murmured, "All this is only if the worst comes to the worst. But I've every confidence that in the clear light of day everything will be cleared up. Let us pray for it, Jack, eh?"

Once more he departed, this time finally, and left Mr. Brett in the impossible situation of having agreed to act as second to both parties because he'd been too cowardly to utter a word in objection.

Indeed, the only soul he'd spoken to with any passion had been the unlucky Tizzy who still wandered, gently sobbing, along the maze of passages and up and down the lurking stairs.

Mercifully the intricate architecture of the Academy's upper part continued to hide her grief from the other wanderers in the night, each of whom pursued his separate winding way like a nightgowned thought in the coils of some dark, gigantic brain.

Suddenly she stopped. Somewhere a door had opened and shut. A breathless silence seemed to fall on all the house. The creakings and gruntings of boards were stilled; then, slowly, but dreadfully sure, came the sound of stealthy steps . . .

Ralph Bunnion, half frightened, half excited by the prospect of the duel, had not gone out that night. Instead, he'd remained in his room, brooding on blood, weapons and cold death upon some gray dawn. Still in his fatal waistcoat, he'd saluted his reflection in the mirror and raised imaginary pistols and swords.

He had almost decided on pistols—one of his friends owned a very fine pair—but still he hesitated. He was not a coward but, if by ill-luck he should fall, a sword thrust was likely to prove less injurious than a pistol shot—which might well be fatal.

He opened a bottle of claret to oil his thoughts. He was very used to claret. At the Old Ship Inn a bottle did no more for him than impart an ease and lightness to his gait. So he drank quite freely and without any sense of care or constraint. The fact that he'd had no supper to lay the claret's foundation, so to speak, had quite slipped his mind; by the time he'd finished half the bottle the ease and lightness that should have tempered his limbs had reached his unsuspecting head.

Matters of life and death slipped effortlessly away and various extraordinary notions, robed in crimson fumes, filled his brain. Lust, anger and the memory of his downland fall inflamed him. In his mind's bleary eye he saw again the tempting, insolent back of Tizzy Alexander whirling away from his outstretched grasp. He clenched his fists and brought them down fiercely on his writing table. Then he drank some more claret to clear his head.

He stood up and stared at himself again in the mirror. For a moment he was shocked at the sight of his injuries; his chiseled features contorted in fury and humiliation. In vain he called up images of his many conquests—saw them fall like painted leaves before the wind of his passion. But always Tizzy interposed with her look of weary disappointment; and again he lived through his frightful fall.

He drank the last of the claret to wash her memory away. But the dangerous fumes within only boiled the more fiercely and his lust and hatred knew no bounds. He snarled and moved vaguely towards the door. If only he could find it, he would move along the corridors like a ghost—like a wolf . . . He would take her in her arrogant bed . . . he would stifle her screams and—

At last he found the door which had unaccountably eluded him. He opened it. Like a wolf towards his wild design, he began to move. Slow, slow . . . but dreadfully sure, his stealthy feet moved on . . .

# 5

THE MOON, THE SAME inquisitive moon that had laid its silver finger on the troubled bed of Mr. Brett, gazed down on the other distracted household in the town—the home of Dr. Harris—as if coldly noting the connection.

Between the two houses lay the silvered windows and phantom

streets from which thieves, murderers and lovers alike all shrank into the concealment of the shadows. But their thoughts and schemes ever ventured abroad, crossing, linking, tangling, till the whole world seemed covered with a web of obscure motives in which even angels might be caught.

The old nurse who had looked after all the Harrises had been the first to scream. She'd gone to wake little Adelaide for her ten o'clock feed.

"Come, little one," she'd crooned. "Come to—"

A beetle-browed infant with hair as black as sin opened its eyes and glared at her. She screamed; she shrieked; she ran distracted out of the room pursued by alien cries from the usurped crib.

Then terror, confusion and frantic grief seized the house till the very cobbles of its walls seemed turned to bulging eyes, all stony with amazement. Every window blazed with light as the Harrises rushed from room to room as if hoping to come upon Adelaide in some unexpected part of the house. Then they went out into the garden and called and rummaged among the bushes; then Dr. Harris ran up and down the street.

Not that anyone had any clear idea of what should be done, but everyone felt they should be doing something—even though, in their heart of hearts, they knew it to be in vain. Several times Dr. Harris went back into the nursery and stared, bewildered, at the crumpled, shrieking infant that lay in his daughter's place. The loss of Adelaide by itself would have been a terrible thing but this substitution—this *change*—was weird and uncanny. It was beyond all normal experience and reasonable explanation. Wretchedly Dr. Harris shook his head. He was a good, learned, persevering sort of man; a man of sense, not given to idle fancy.

"For pity's sake, *do* something!" wept his wife. "Look again before it's too late!"

"Too late for what?"

"I don't know—I don't know!"

So once again Dr. Harris joined in the despairing search; and, of all that troubled household, the most eager, the most urgent and the most anxious to look and look again was the only son, young Harris himself. It was he who was ever in the forefront, full of hopes, ideas and sudden sights that, alas, came to nought. It was he who thought he saw Adelaide at the bottom of the garden; it was he who thought he saw her in the attic.

Deep and subtle consideration had suggested this course to Harris as being the most brilliant way to avoid suspicion. His absence from the scene, or even his lagging behind, would surely have seemed unusual and so might have led to the horror of discovery. So he threw himself into the search with extraordinary vigor and invention. But all the while, under this dazzling counterfeit, his brain was steadily at work.

At last it became tragically plain to the family that Adelaide was not going to be found; and, in spite of the younger Harris's urgent entreaties that they should look just once more, they gathered wearily in the front parlor to decide on what next should be done.

"Bostock," said Dr. Harris gravely. "I'll have to call Bostock."

At this, the son of the house started in horrible alarm, till he understood that his father had meant Bostock the sea captain—his friend's parent—who was a Justice of the Peace. So Captain Bostock was fetched from his bed and informed of the unnatural disaster that had struck at the home of Dr. Harris.

He listened, yawning and frowning the while and fixing his

piercing blue eyes upon one member of the family after another as they broke in with uncontrollable agitation. This gaze of his which, in its day, had subdued mutinous sailors and almost the sea itself, had the effect of calming the parlor. Everyone dropped their eyes; but not the younger Harris whose mounting dread of discovery would have given him strength to outstare St. Peter himself. He sat and glared, with terrible fixity, at Captain Bostock, being entirely convinced that one turn of his head would reveal its guilty contents. Then, little by little, as the sea captain talked, his dread diminished and his brain resumed its underground activity.

Though Captain Bostock was, as he himself freely admitted, a sturdy, straightforward and even blunt fellow, many years on the Bench had taught him a great deal. He was, he owned with a sigh, no stranger to the webs of deceit in which men raveled themselves. In his time he had come upon many affairs as curious as the disappearance of Adelaide. He did not say this with any idea of belittling the Harris family's grief, but merely to establish an authority over it.

None the less Mrs. Harris looked plainly resentful at what she took to be Captain Bostock's insinuation that they were all making a great fuss over nothing. The sea captain, anxious to correct the false impression, hastily admitted that there were certain aspects of the Adelaide affair that distinguished it from the commonplace.

In his opinion—for what it was worth—it was not so much the disappearance of Adelaide that was extraordinary, but the *appearance* of the unknown infant in her place. He took it for granted, he said, in view of his long friendship with Dr. Harris, that the family were not mistaken and the infant was not their own. Here Mrs. Harris could not be restrained from telling the sea captain that his long friendship with Dr. Harris might go to the Devil; a mother knew what was her own child and what was not, and that the new-comer was a male infant which, somehow or another, seemed to her the worst thing of all. Then she began to sob and Captain Bostock said, "Madam, madam," several times in an effort to atone for his unlucky remark. At last Mrs. Harris was brought to a temporary calm and Captain Bostock admitted cautiously that the situation was one that called for an inquiry of *peculiar* delicacy . . .

The younger Harris's heart leaped and thundered. The very word "inquiry" tolled like the bell of doom inside his breast. Nor was what followed any less alarming. He sat, cold and deathly, as the consequences of his and Bostock's experiment in Natural History grew and grew till it was like a monster whose tentacles reached into every corner of the living world.

Naturally, Captain Bostock would institute inquiries (that terrible word again!)—and here he tapped the side of his weathered nose down which ran a neat, straight scar—but he would advise Dr. Harris to take certain steps himself.

At the Old Ship Inn there happened to be staying a certain Mr. Raven—Mr. Selwyn Raven. Had Dr. Harris heard of him? Well, well, perhaps not. Unless one had cause, one did not hear of such as Mr. Raven. Such persons are rather more discreet than most. The nature of their trade is against advertisement. None the less, in his, Captain Bostock's opinion, for what it was worth, the Harrises could do no better than consult Mr. Raven whose reputation, among those who had cause to know it, stood very high indeed for pursuing inquiries of *peculiar* delicacy. There could be little doubt that Mr. Raven, once in possession of the facts, would quickly arrive at the truth.

At the word "truth," the younger Harris's blood all but congealed. He felt like some rare and lovely creature caught in a forest of implacable hunters seeking to destroy him. He twisted, he turned, he darted this way and that in the secret places of his mind to escape. But outwardly, by reason of his almost superhuman strength of character, he appeared quite still, and with an air of utter calm. There was a small, remote part of Harris that was able to observe this, and even to admire it.

At last Captain Bostock rose to go and Harris, still brilliantly counterfeiting an inward peace, courteously offered to attend him. He had reached a conclusion and determined on a course of action.

For a moment Captain Bostock fixed him with his piercing eyes which seemed to go right inside Harris's head, but apparently he saw nothing there for he patted the lad's arm and suffered him to lead the way to the neighboring street.

Harris waited for the sea captain to shut his front door, then, with easy stealth, he floated round to the back of the house and summoned his friend by means of a stone at his window. Bostock appeared, disappeared, then appeared again and came looping down through an ancient apple tree that grew against the house, pausing only to embrace Jupiter, his brutish ginger cat who waited on a bough for some necessary bird.

The friends shook hands; then Harris told Bostock about the consternation in the Harris household and the mention of the man who was staying at the Old Ship—the inquiry agent, Mr. Selwyn Raven. Bostock looked at Harris in terror. He could see Harris was alarmed; and to him Harris's alarm was as the cracking of a temple or the shaking of a star in the sky.

"But I've thought of something, old friend," whispered Harris reassuringly; in a curious way, Bostock's simplicity seemed to reassure both of them. Bostock's great faith gave Harris confidence, and the more confidence Harris displayed, the greater grew Bostock's faith. There was really no limit to it all. "I think I know where she is."

"Who?"

"Adelaide. I've put two and two together, Bosty—and there's only one answer."

"What's that, Harris?" breathed Bostock, who was not strong on Arithmetic.

"She's back in the school."

"How do you know?"

"Human nature, Bosty."

Bostock frowned; he did not like to question Harris, particularly about human nature.

"Mark my words, Bosty, at this very minute my sister's asleep at the school, snug in Miss Alexander's bed."

"Then—then Ralph took her all the way back again?"

Harris tapped the side of his nose. "Human nature, old friend. He fancied Miss Alexander; Miss Alexander fancied Adelaide. Two and two, Bosty."

"Human nature," nodded Bostock, but with a note of uncertainty in his voice. Then Harris smiled and Bostock was reassured.

"Let's go, Bosty."

"Where, Harris?"

"To the school. We've got to get her back, you know. It wouldn't be natural to leave her."

"Right now, Harris?"

"Right now, old friend. Safest and best. They'll all be asleep at the school. After all, what can have happened to keep *them* awake?"

The moon stood in the sky above the two distracted households like a scimitar: it illumined a thread between them like a silver worm winding through a world of black. Along this thread, which here and there vanished under interrupting shadows, moved the double shape of Bostock and Harris and, a little way behind, a smaller, quicker shape that stopped and started, then went arrow straight.

The brutish Jupiter had left the birdless apple tree to follow his master into the night.

"Go back!" pleaded Bostock at intervals, and Jupiter would pause and stare at him meaningfully; then, when the friends went on, he would follow after with the quick, stiff-legged walk of an elderly but still powerful cat, no longer able to hunt for himself but eager for others to oblige.

Though the two friends were as familiar with the way to Dr. Bunnion's as with each other's pockets, it now became mysterious and uncanny. The solemnity of the night and the desperate nature of their journey lent an unearthly aspect to the well-worn streets. The houses—now the tombs of sleep—seemed curiously insubstantial, as if their very walls had only been bodied forth by the dreams within and a touch would dissolve them into wide vistas . . .

But Bostock and Harris were real. No dream could have bodied them forth, and no touch could have dissolved them. They crept among the shadowy plots of half-built houses where ambitious builders were extending the scope of the town. Stealthily they removed a ladder and carried it with them until they reached the school.

All was in darkness. The Academy was wrapped round and round in a deep silence. Harris pointed upwards. Miss Alexander's room lay under the roof at the side of the house. The mystery of the Academy's upper architecture was as an open book to a mind like Harris's.

Harris smiled. The window was open to the warm night. He nodded. Nature herself was on the side of the two friends. Cautiously the ladder was raised and settled against the wall. Harris signed to Bostock to mount while he steadied the ladder's foot.

Bostock shook hands with Harris and began to mount. As he did so, a rapid shape passed Harris. Jupiter, with hungry green eyes, had gone up after his master. Harris saw them enter the window almost together, with Jupiter scrambling over Bostock's shoulder.

Harris waited. For a moment there was silence. Then there was a loud and dreadful cry followed by the sound of something heavy falling. Then Jupiter reappeared and descended the ladder at a great speed with Bostock after him. Bostock looked very white. Harris paused till Bostock was down, then the two friends fled for their lives. They did not stop running until they were back in Bostock's garden. There they leaned against the apple tree while, in the branches above them, Jupiter cleaned the blood from his claws.

A terrible thing had happened. Inflamed by vengeance, lust and wine, Ralph Bunnion had accomplished his monstrous errand. Unseen by the other wanderers in the night, he had somehow unraveled the maze of passages, stairs and corners and found out

Tizzy Alexander's room. A wolfish smile had disfigured his handsome features. Quietly he'd opened the door. Then had struck disaster. The bed was empty; but the room was not. A shape of strange, inhuman aspect was at the window. Outlined against the sky it seemed, to Ralph's crimsoned mind, to be part man and part beast; from its human shoulders reared the wicked head of a cat.

Courageously he'd stumbled forward, hands outstretched. He was in such a mood to attack angels and devils alike. He reached out—and for a second time the concerns of Bostock and Harris crossed the purpose of the headmaster's son.

The brutish Jupiter flew at the intruder in the darkened room, savaged his face and fled, hissing with alarm; nor was Bostock far behind. Ralph Bunnion shrieked and fell with a sound like thunder. The house shook, and the wanderers in the night came rushing upon the scene before there was any chance of escape.

They found him lying drunkenly beside Tizzy Alexander's tumbled bed; and even in the uncertain candlelight it was plain there had been further damage done to his unlucky face. Denial—even if he'd been in a condition to make one—would have been hopeless, and the little Academy quaked in the grip of confusion, anger and fear.

Events which, by skill, compromise and goodwill might have been halted, were now whirled out of all sensible men's control on their fatal course of calamity. Dr. Bunnion could no longer uphold the innocence of his moaning, bleeding son; and Major Alexander did not see how he could avoid avenging his daughter's honor.

Shortly before dawn, when Mr. Brett had at last managed to forget his own wretched situation sufficiently to fall into a light sleep, he was awakened by yet another knocking at his door. Savagely he cried out, "Go away! For God's sake, leave me in peace! All of you, go to Hell!"

Outside the door, poor, bewildered Tizzy Alexander sobbed quietly and went away.

# 6

THE BELLS OF ST. NICHOLAS'S wrinkled the morning air as they summoned the town to prayer. Dully the two distressed households understood it to be Sunday and they must needs carry their griefs and perplexities to church to thank God for being alive.

"Let us pray," suggested Mr. Hudson, the vicar, when the time came; and the congregation knelt—some opening their hearts for relief from private anguish and others endeavouring to close them against the prying eyes of the Almighty. Chief among the former were Mrs. Harris and Tizzy Alexander; and chief among the latter were Bostock and Harris.

Not even God can help me now, thought Harris, as he peered round the well-filled pews for a sight of Ralph Bunnion who, it turned out, had been the last living soul to clap eyes on Adelaide and had left her only he knew where. After the night's disaster, it was plain that Adelaide was not in the school. Harris had some confused notion of throwing himself on the school hero's mercy, confessing all (or nearly all) and imploring his aid. But Ralph Bunnion was nowhere to be seen.

Sadly Harris glanced sideways to where the sturdy Bostock knelt with closed eyes and open mouth. He envied his friend his slow, simple mind that was not tormented with dreadful thoughts. Though Bostock might never reach the heights that he, Harris, sometimes knew, he would never plummet to the depths that he, Harris, was now in.

A great loneliness fell upon Harris as round about him prayers of all descriptions rose in silence to the church's roof. He felt himself to be the outcast of creation against whom every man's hand was raised. Then he looked at Bostock again and was briefly consoled. Bostock was his companion and friend; he was just as involved as Harris himself and would, therefore, be bound to suffer at his side. At once Harris felt less lonely and more a part of the common fate of mankind.

Mr. Hudson nodded to his flock. He was a shaggy man with large hands and large feet and, as he began to snap and bark his sermon from the pulpit, was the very image of a pious sheepdog with a sharp eye for strays.

As the town was becoming quite fashionable of late by reason of an interest in sea-bathing, Mr. Hudson thought it necessary to touch on the extreme difficulty of rich men entering the Kingdom of Heaven unaided. The poor were all right—here he smiled encouragingly at the fisherfolk at the back—but the rich—here he frowned at the private pews—stood in need of assistance. Though he didn't say it outright, he implied pretty strongly that they weren't likely to get such assistance from God direct; their only chance lay through the proper channels. That was what churches were for. And St. Nicholas's in particular. They were not likely to do better elsewhere even though the actual building stood in need of repair. Exposed as it was to the winds from the sea, even the house of God was subject to the elements. The roof leaked. Money was required to restore it. And where should such money come from? From those who would benefit. From this very congregation who prayed and expected their prayers to be answered.

Here Mr. Hudson paused so that the equity of the arrangement might sink in. Harris felt in his pockets and wondered how much he could afford on the chance of a quick return. He had reached the final pit of despair in which anything was worth trying.

He had a shilling and a sixpence. Strenuously he wrestled with his conscience, arguing that Mr. Hudson would never know that if he gave the sixpence, a shilling had been withheld. But God would know, said a pious voice within. "Yah!" snarled Harris, whose faith was a rubbery commodity and tended to shift out of the way under pressure. "Who cares?"

He fished in his pockets and came upon a battered brass button that a horse had trodden flat. He mused; why the sixpence when the button would make as good a noise in the collecting box? After all, it was the thought that counted—and Mr. Hudson would certainly *think* it was money.

When the service ended, Harris frowned and dropped the button in the box. The vicar smiled and wagged his clasped hands behind his back; and Bostock, seeing Harris's gesture, sighed and put in a shilling, which was all he had.

"Well!" said Harris, challenging the great host of heaven. "Now show me You're really there! Where's Adelaide?"

The congregation had left the cool shadows of the church and were out in the pagan sunshine.

"Answer me!" muttered Harris, looking up defiantly at the golden pastures of the universe. "Or You'll be the loser!"

Thus Harris barbed his soul and aimed it at the sky—to bring down an angel; or nothing. That he himself had not been absolutely honest in this trial of faith did not disturb him in the least. On the contrary, he argued with Jesuitical subtlety, the Almighty now had every opportunity for displaying His vaunted understanding and forgiveness.

He waited while round about he heard the clatter of gossip and the salty grumbling of fisherfolk as the Sunday town, in homespun and starfish ribbons, jostled him out of their homeward way. But nothing came to him from the invisible God. Instead, sturdily stamping across the graveyard, came Bostock. He had left his family, gone out of his way to raise his hat, with furious blushes, to the wild slender Miss Harris, and come to join his friend.

Harris, who was at the very crisis of belief, looked depressed, and Bostock wondered how he might cheer him up. He did not like to see Harris miserable.

"I expect she'll turn up somewhere, Harris," he mumbled, and laid his hand timidly on his friend's narrow shoulder.

Harris turned. "Bosty, old friend," he whispered. "There ain't no God."

The words struck Bostock like a blow in the stomach. They were so strange and unexpected.

"The sky's empty, old friend," went on Harris grimly. "There's just us, Bosty."

"What, you and me?" Bostock was shaken to the depths of his soul.

"No," said Harris irritably. "Mankind. All of us down here. We're all there is, Bosty. The rest is—is air."

"Are you sure, Harris?" asked Bostock pleadingly. He knew he hadn't the intellect to question his friend, but at the same time he did not want to abandon his own beliefs without a struggle. They meant a great deal to him, and had it been anyone else but wise old Harris who'd shaken them, he'd have clouted him without more ado. "How—how do you *know?*"

Harris frowned. He did not care to admit that his reason was chiefly that he'd received no answer to his gift of the brass button.

"But there *must* be a God," urged Bostock desperately.

"Why, old friend?"

"Because—because of everything. Look about you, Harris! All the grass and trees and different animals and flowers. Who made them if not God?"

"Somebody else," said Harris bleakly. The friends stared at one another, Harris as still and somber as the headstones among which they stood, and Bostock swaying slightly as if rocking in a sea of doubt. Bostock turned his small, fierce eyes from side to side, ranging the wide landscape as if trying to see in it some other light than the bright sun's. Painfully he stared from the soft, silken sea to the green, velvet folds of the Downs. Not two miles off he saw the tiny village of Preston clustering like a brood of kittens about the wise gray church whose square head watched over the cottages, ready to call them back if they strayed into danger. Bostock's eyes began to fill with tears. Passionately he struggled to reject Harris's grim philosophy and to bring his friend back into the warm, motherly world.

"Look, Harris—look!" he muttered, pointing to the village but unable to put his thoughts into words.

Wearily Harris looked. "What is it, old friend?"

"The—the church," said Bostock incoherently, and hoped Harris would understand.

Harris gazed at the aged building that looked, from where he stood, to be no better than a child's toy. "Poor, poor Bosty," he whispered pityingly. He was half sorry for the damage he'd done his friend, but nevertheless the truth was more sacred than anything else; nothing was worse than worshiping a lie. Just how Harris, whose mind was furtive in the extreme, managed to believe in this philosophy, was a mystery as deep as life; but then he was a scientist.

"Yes, Bosty—another church."

He stopped. His heart quickened. *Another* church. In his mind's eye he saw once more the horseman and the baby of the previous night, and in a blaze of understanding he guessed what had happened. Ralph Bunnion, with Adelaide in his arms, for some reason or another must have ridden *past* St. Nicholas's and on to the church at Preston!

The lights came on in his eyes. He thumped Bostock on the back. "*Now* I know, old friend!"

"I don't want to hear it," said Bostock bitterly—thinking Harris had shifted the heavens still further afield.

"He took her to Preston," said Harris. "*That*'s where Adelaide went!"

"Oh," said Bostock. "I thought you meant God."

"What's God got to do with it? Come on, Bosty!"

He set off at a smart trot towards Preston and Bostock followed after. All questions of faith and belief had vanished from Harris's mind. He left the gates of Heaven swinging open, so to speak, for God to resume. His leasehold until he, Harris, chose to foreclose again.

When the friends reached Preston, Harris's inspiration was confirmed. Ingeniously they fell into conversation with a boy and learned that a baby had indeed been left in the church on the previous night. But almost at once their lifted hopes were dashed to the ground. They were too late. The baby had already been taken to the poorhouse in Brighton.

As they walked back in the deepest dejection, the fleeting thought struck Harris that had he put his shilling, or even his sixpence, in the collecting box instead of the brass button, they might have been in time. Then he shook his head. No god could be *that* petty.

"At least we know where she is," said Bostock hopefully, and secretly considered the shilling he'd sacrificed in church had been money well spent. Of such strange material is faith built, unbuilt and built again—in ever-changing designs.

By the time the two friends drew near their homes, they were buoyant again. Harris's eyes were gleaming and Bostock watched him admiringly. He knew that Harris's large brain was fairly humming to devise a plan to rescue Adelaide from the poorhouse. He did not anticipate any further problems.

They shook hands at the corner of Harris's street and parted, each confident that their troubles were all but at an end. Harris was whistling under his breath and, as he entered his house, his spindly, wrinkle-stockinged legs did a jaunty, doorstep jig.

"This is my son, sir," said Dr. Harris wearily as Harris entered the parlor, and the stranger smiled.

He was shortish, stout and quietly dressed. He wore a neat bagwig and had soft, large eyes. With an unaccountable chill, Harris saw he had a clubbed foot whose grim black bulk seemed to belie the gentleness of his expression.

"This is Mr. Selwyn Raven," said Dr. Harris to his suddenly pale son. "He has come to get at the truth about Adelaide."

# 7

"A SAD AFFAIR, my young friend," said Mr. Raven. Harris nodded warily, his eyes moving from Mr. Raven's mild face to his unnatural black boot.

"I don't wish to pry, young man, into any of your private secrets, but a few questions, if you'd be so kind, eh?" He nodded to Dr. Harris who looked momentarily distressed—as if on his son's behalf—then hurriedly left the room.

Harris felt curiously abandoned. He did not know what to make of Mr. Raven who kept shifting his wicked boot as if to draw attention to it.

"You are interested in such things?" asked the inquiry agent, observing Harris's fascination. "But of course! Being a physician's son such deformities must seem commonplace."

Harris nodded and smiled casually. Or believed that he did.

"Would you care to see it?" offered Mr. Raven eagerly. He bent down as if to remove the boot.

"No!" said Harris quickly. He had been seized by a sudden dread that the deformed foot might have been something altogether frightful. Mr. Raven looked mildly surprised and apologized for embarrassing the young gentleman. He had not intended to do any such thing, but when one had such a misfortune it was difficult to judge its effect. He himself had always found it was better to be open with it . . . not to attempt to hide it, or even to pretend it wasn't there. After all, it was an act of God and one didn't deny God—

"You do believe in God, young man?" he asked anxiously; and then, before the startled Harris could reply, he smiled and added, "But of course. You've just come from church. When did you last see your sister?"

"I—I don't remember," said Harris faintly. The abrupt change of direction made him break out in a sweat. Mr. Raven was an eerie adversary.

"I didn't mean to pry into your religious beliefs, young man," said Mr. Raven gently. "But I like to know where we stand." Again he moved his horrible boot as if, having discovered exactly where Harris was standing, he intended to flatten him under it. "Did you see any stranger in the neighborhood yesterday? A woman, perhaps?"

Again the abrupt change of direction; but this time Harris was ready. "Yes!" he said quickly; he was anxious to transfer Mr. Raven's attention to someone else.

"Interesting," said the inquiry agent; but strangely did not pursue the point. Instead he rapped his boot sharply with a stout stick that had been leaning beside his chair. He chuckled disarmingly and explained that the deformed member was inclined to "go to sleep," and he liked to wake it up from time to time . . .

Harris began to feel sick. He longed for Mr. Raven to go; he was morbidly terrified of him. Now Mr. Raven was asking him if he knew of any enemies the household had; a dismissed servant, perhaps . . . ? Fiercely Harris retreated within himself. You're a genius, Harris! he screamed in his heart. And he's a—a madman! You are more than a match for him. Outwit him! Be calm! Smile! Answer him; don't be rushed! For God's sake, be careful! None the less, in spite of the certainty of his own intellectual superiority over this man, Harris could not keep down a terrible desire to confess to Mr. Raven and so get rid of him. I took her! he longed to shout out. Bostock and me! We took her!

He felt the words rattling in his throat. He coughed and swallowed to keep them to himself.

"This strange woman you saw," said Mr. Raven smoothly. "Can you describe her?"

"What woman?" said Harris, bewildered by the suddenness of the question.

"Oh nothing. I must have been mistaken. Only I thought you said you saw such a one in the neighborhood. I must have misheard you. Pardon me."

Harris bit his lip. He'd slipped. The devilish Mr. Raven had caught him out. All desire to confess vanished under a flood of panic.

"No matter," murmured the inquiry agent, hobbling to his feet. "I shall be at the Old Ship Inn. If anything occurs to you—if you remember anything you think might interest me—come and see me. I shall be waiting, my young friend . . . any time, any time . . ."

With that, he clumped from the room and was presently out of the house.

The inquiry agent limped along the street, his stick and his great boot tapping and thumping inquisitively on the ground, as if searching for a weakness or a symptom of rot. Mostly he kept his eyes downwards, but from time to time he glanced at the houses he passed and then up to the splendid sun. And, as always, his eyes remained mild, and his expression innocent. It was only his boot—his monstrous boot—that suggested Mr. Raven was a formidable man.

He was deeply acquainted with the darknesses of the human soul, and he knew too well the terror of the guilty spirit as it twists and turns to escape. Suspicion was second nature to him; and he had no first. Wearily he brooded on his last interview—with the boy Harris whose spirit had fled almost visibly for refuge to his boots.

The inquiry agent shrugged his shoulders. He was all too used to being greeted with fear and guilt. Where was innocence? A dream—a milky idea in the noddles of fools, and nowhere else. It was not even in the hearts of children, all of whom had their corrupting little secrets which they struggled to hide from the light of day.

What had the boy Harris been trying to hide with his frowns and grins, his rapid, sideways eyes and his dismal attempts at honesty of manner? A theft from a neighbor, perhaps? Or a furtive tryst with some sluttish maid, et cetera?

The expression "et cetera" was a very necessary one to Mr. Raven. It was like a great black bag in which he tumbled men's thoughts and deeds when he sensed they were too deep and foul for other words.

Mr. Raven knew it all. Nothing surprised him anymore. Guilt was in every heart; even infants in their cradles tended to look fearful and evasive when Mr. Raven stared mildly down on them. The gypsy child in the Harris's usurped cot had crumpled its face and turned from the inquiry agent's bland eyes as if suddenly conscious of the original sin that had dealt it, like the Ace of Spades, into the frightened household's hand.

"Yes, my young friend," Mr. Raven had whispered. "*You* know—and soon, very soon, so shall I."

At length he reached the Old Ship Inn where he asked for a mutton chop and a pint of sherry to be sent up to his room; the Harrises had not seen fit to ask him to luncheon. Not that the omission rankled particularly, but Mr. Raven had noted it. He sat by his window and stared out on to the smooth Sunday sea and considered the strange affair of Adelaide Harris. Or, rather, the strange affair of the mysterious baby that now lay in her place; it was glaringly clear that Adelaide had only been removed to make way for it. The Harrises were ordinary folk and, however they might have rated themselves, Mr. Raven knew they were of no consequence in the world; so their infant could have been of no value to anyone. Its only possession was the space it had occupied—its cot; and *this* it was, rather than the infant itself, that had been stolen. For the dark one . . . for the dark one . . .

The importance of the black-haired baby fascinated and tantalized him. "What secret lust begot you, my young friend?" he murmured to himself. "And what shameful womb nourished you, et cetera? Discover that, and we discover all!" He rapped his boot with his stick as if seeking confirmation.

Indeed, it was almost as though he conversed with his monstrous appendage and received from it answers as black as itself. "Was it your mother or your father who passed on the telltale gypsy blood?"

Before there could be an answer, his sherry and mutton chop came in at the door on a tray carried by the boot-boy since none of the maids would venture into Mr. Raven's room.

The boy put the tray down and glanced inquisitively at the inquiry agent's boot and wondered if he ever took it off. Night after night there was only the commonplace right one left out to be cleaned. The great ugly left boot never appeared but on Mr. Raven's foot. The boy went out and Mr. Raven ate his chop and continued to worry at the problem.

Two things were plain. The gypsy baby must have been important enough for it to have been laid in a private cot rather than entrusted to the stony mercy of some church night; and there must have been a traitor in the Harris household to have opened doors—and closed them afterwards.

The inquiry agent washed down the mutton chop with the sherry and returned to staring out of the window from which he could see the quiet sea endlessly unrolling on the shingle like some wide, secret document displaying itself, then drawing back with a whisper before it could be read.

"What is it saying?" murmured Mr. Raven, tapping his boot.

That there is nothing so black as the human heart, came the answer. Under the sea lie poisoned bones and ribs all chipped by knives. Bullets roll inside skulls and ghastly captains lash long-dead cabin boys with whips of trailing weeds, et cetera. Yet the sea's surface is as bland and fair as a baby's cheek . . . So plunge deep, Selwyn Raven, and deeper yet till you reach the gloomy depths where human motives coil and strike. For every action there is a foul motive—and this it is your sacred task to find.

"Alas!" whispered Mr. Raven, gazing down on his boot with a mixture of fear and repugnance. "Were it not for you I might not be cursed with such bitter knowledge. I too might be blind like other men and not be burdened with such truth. Before this affair of Adelaide Harris is done with, great families will totter and guilty souls will plunge into Hell. Murder may be done, et cetera . . ."

So it was that, with these thoughts in his mind, he clumped from his room and went downstairs to the back parlor where sherry and claret were loosening devious tongues and unlocking tangled hearts. Secrets black, secrets gray, all came to the ears of Selwyn Raven as he sat and listened and distilled them into the bitter draft of guilt.

# 8

RALPH BUNNION, having risen at last from his bed and taken a cautious lunch, was on his way to meet a friend. He walked carefully, for the effects of the calamitous night had not entirely worn off. His face was deathly pale and the double scratches had gone black and venomous-looking—as if some dissatisfied artist had made an attempt to cross him out. None the less he was dressed with his usual care, wearing a dark blue coat cut away to display a lavish waistcoat embroidered with the yellow and purple flowerets of love-in-idleness. Maggie Hemp had stitched it for him during a lull in the first weeks of their passion and had woven her name into the design.

Sunday walkers, crossing his path, glanced curiously at him but he returned a look of dignified aloofness and glided on. In his own way, Ralph Bunnion was something of a hero. Though he knew Major Alexander's accusation to be false and the challenge therefore unjust, he scorned to say so . . . partly because he knew he wouldn't be believed and partly because the notion of a duel was grandly romantic.

A great many noble and even tragic ideas thronged his brain and he tended to look on the passing landscape as bidding its last farewell to the gay and dashing Ralph. Already he'd determined, if he should fall, that he would bequeath his collection of waistcoats to Frederick.

Frederick was the friend he was meeting, and it was he who owned the pair of dueling pistols. Ralph would certainly have preferred swords, but in the end it turned out that he didn't know anybody who had a pair and it seemed undignified to hire them. So pistols it was to be, with Frederick as his second.

Or one of his seconds. Ralph frowned. His father had gone and saddled him with that sly, sour fellow Brett as the other. Ralph disliked Mr. Brett, and it was humiliating to be seconded by him. But there was no help for it now. Brett was to fix up about the surgeon, and there again his father had interfered. Sometimes Ralph wondered who it was who was supposed to be fighting the duel. His father insisted on having Dr. Harris whose brat was at the school. He fancied this might keep things in the family, as it were, and prevent them from getting out all over the town.

An expression of melancholy contempt came over Ralph's face.

What good could even Dr. Harris do when the glorious Ralph lay quiet and still with only his red blood moving, moving away from a hole in his breast?

Ralph's heart beat rapidly. Why did he always think of himself as being dead? Was it an omen? "What will be, will be," he whispered philosophically—and entered the Old Ship Inn.

There were few people in the dim back parlor where Ralph and his friends delighted to hold court and sing and drink the night into day, but good old Frederick was among them. He was thinner than Ralph and would need to fill out before the waistcoats would fit him. Ralph shivered as once again his thoughts implied his own death.

"Arternoon, Mister Ralph, sir," said the landlord affably. "Pint of the usual?"

"Half," said Ralph quietly. "Just a half, landlord."

"Night on the tiles, eh?" chuckled the landlord; then, observing Ralph's savaged face, guffawed loudly as the full extent of his own wit reached him. "He—he! I sees you been tom-catting again! Lord, Mister Ralph, you'll have the town on your tail afore long!"

Though privately the landlord detested Ralph Bunnion and his gaudy friends, they were entitled to his courtesy as they drank well and kept the parlor from being lonely. Ralph smiled feebly at the landlord's tribute, then joined the negligent Frederick at a table by the fireplace.

"Rattlin' fine mess your face is in, old dear," said Frederick, yawning sympathetically. "Tell us all. Your uncle Fred's all ears." This last was not entirely a figure of speech. He did have rather large ears—or else a very small face—and they stuck out from under his wig like loosened coach wheels. Otherwise he was presentable enough, being the son of a successful livery-stable owner.

"Fred," said Ralph with a seriousness that caused his friend to abandon his smile, "I need your pistols—"

Suddenly Ralph stopped. He had become aware of a stranger watching him. He frowned, and the stranger's innocent eyes seemed to drift away under pressure of his own. This stranger was a stoutish, plainly dressed man; he was quite ordinary, even pleasant-looking, but for his left foot which was encased in a gigantic black boot. Ralph shuddered. There was something horrible about that boot and the way it seemed to crouch beside the commonplace right one like some silent, evil hound.

"What's up?" asked Frederick. Ralph shook his head, then went on talking but in a much subdued voice. The stranger half closed his eyes and leaned forward imperceptibly. From time to time Ralph glanced at him with a kind of fearful disgust—at which the stranger would ease himself back and seem to transfer his attention elsewhere, where it would be equally unwelcome.

"So that's how it stands," muttered Ralph, having explained the whole wretched story as he saw it, and confided his fears for the immediate future. "If I don't do for her cursed pa, sure as anything the brute will do for me. But come what may, I won't be black-mailed into marrying his tatty little slut."

Ralph was very violent against Tizzy whom he blamed for everything. He swallowed down the remainder of his claret and the landlord, unasked, sent his boy to replenish it. Ralph, feeling rather warm, removed his coat and Frederick gazed with gloomy admiration at the splendid waistcoat. Even the clubfooted stranger seemed impressed by it and Ralph lounged back carelessly. The stranger peered, and smiled . . .

The parlor door opened and a newcomer entered. He was slim, no more than twenty-eight, with a thin, worried-looking face. Though not fashionably dressed, his linen was clean and neatly mended. He glanced about the parlor uneasily.

This, thought Mr. Selwyn Raven, is a man who is haunted by a secret. Mr. Raven, to the landlord's disapproval, had been in the back parlor for some hours over a single glass of brandy and water. During that time, a little world of mean sins and cheap corruption had passed in review before him. Silently he'd sat and listened as they'd come and gone: faithless husbands, dishonored wives and false friends, all winding in and out of their tapestries of lies. But what he sought still eluded him. Then the haunted newcomer had come in and Mr. Raven had shifted his ominous boot. This man carries a load of guilt such as Judas Iscariot must have carried, thought Mr. Raven idly. His eyes widened as he saw the newcomer make for the two young men who'd mentioned pistols and blackmail.

"Why if it isn't Mr. Brett," said Ralph Bunnion sourly, and introduced Frederick to his other second.

Mr. Brett sat down with a furtive glance round the parlor as if expecting Major Alexander to appear and confront him with his wretched duplicity. He'd had an abominable morning in which he'd flitted from room to room in the school to avoid the Major and the Bunnions. Luncheon had been worse, with the headmaster saying grace as if it was a graveside prayer over the invisible body of his son or his Arithmetic master; then had followed a silent meal laced with such looks as might have cut the beef far better than the knives. Next, Major Alexander had caught him in the privy and earnestly reminded him of his obligations as his second, claimed his loyalty, his honor, his soul and, it seemed to the unhappy Mr.

Brett, his eternal life—and told him that the duel, unless anything happened to prevent it, would take place upon the following Saturday. He didn't see how he could postpone it any longer.

Shortly after that the Bunnions, father and son, had trapped him in the passage outside his classroom and, looking threateningly over him, had claimed much the same degree of loyalty as had the Major before them. The one had followed so closely upon the other that it seemed extraordinary to Mr. Brett that the Bunnions couldn't still hear the Major's words. At last, by desperate nods and reckless promises he'd escaped them—only to see the fiery little Major beckoning him from the stairs.

"When you call on Bunnion's second," he'd urged, "tell him we're open to reason!"

Bunnion's second. That was him. "My principal's open to reason," muttered Mr. Brett to himself in a quiet corner—and half waited on a reply. To his overwrought mind it seemed that there must be at least two James Bretts; but alas, neither was an improvement on the other. Too well he knew that all his separate selves were made of the same weak clay.

Then he saw Bunnion *père* shambling towards him, his enormous eyes gleaming with *second* thoughts. Panic seized Mr. Brett. The school seemed full of Bunnions and Alexanders. Wherever he turned they appeared, from corner, door, stair, from the very shadows; smiling, beckoning, plucking at him, drawing him nearer and nearer to that moment of exposure when he would be revealed as an object of universal contempt and distrust. And in that universe would be Tizzy, her eyes out-flashing a sky-full of stars.

The headmaster was almost upon him when he saw Sorley, the fat boarder, passing on his way to the kitchen. "Sorley!" cried Mr.

Brett, and clutched fiercely at the boy who stared from master to master with slow alarm. Dr. Bunnion patted Sorley on the head. Not for worlds would he have brought up the scandal of his son and Major Alexander in Sorley's presence. Mr. Brett knew it and for the next hour or so took to following the baronet's son everywhere, thus driving the fat boarder into a truly pitiable state of guilt for he knew not what.

"We must be discreet!" said Mr. Brett as he seated himself between Ralph and Frederick and gazed from one to the other in a dazed kind of way. Dr. Bunnion's last words to him had been concerned with the overwhelming need for discretion. Ralph's whole future was in the balance; a word out of place could wreck it. After all, the Sorleys of Cuckfield would scarcely be pleased to connect themselves with a scandal. It was more to Frederick than to Ralph that Mr. Brett addressed his words in the hope of impressing him with Dr. Bunnion's fears and Ralph's marital hopes. "Because of the Sorleys, you understand," murmured Mr. Brett.

"The Sorleys," mused Frederick. "Ain't that Sir Walter Sorley of Cuckfield?"

In his father's livery-stable business, Frederick had made himself master of a real directory of titled names. It was his only intellectual accomplishment and he was fond of displaying it.

"No need to shout," said Ralph, uncomfortably aware of the stranger with the club foot whose large, innocent eyes seemed fastened to his magnificent waistcoat-like buttons on abnormally long threads. "I suppose the other second will be calling on you any time now," he went on, turning to Mr. Brett who nodded eerily. "And then you'll be seeing about Dr. Harris? What the—"

Suddenly there'd come a sharp scraping noise from the direction of the stranger. His boot had moved forward and remained, swaying slightly, as if straining on a leash. Then the stranger, observing all eyes upon him, smiled apologetically, finished his brandy and water, and clumped out of the parlor.

"Good riddance!" muttered the landlord under his breath.


Mr. Selwyn Raven's vigil had at last been rewarded. He had heard what he'd been waiting for: the connection between one secret and another. He had found the telltale thread that, sooner or later, would lead him to the center of the weird labyrinth in which the mystery of Adelaide Harris was concealed. He went back up to his room to fit the pieces of the puzzle together in his mind.

One tiny thing, the unguarded mention of a single name, had illuminated everything. Dr. Harris. The inquiry agent sat down by the window and patiently recalled the fragments of talk he'd overheard. Blackmail, pistols, forced marriages, a Sussex baronet and then, like a key turning in these dark wards, the single name of Dr. Harris; the fatal connection.

"Tom-catting again, Mister Ralph?" The landlord's words recurred, and with them, the image of the young man, lounging back in his chair, displaying his ridiculous floral waistcoat. "Maggie Hemp!" whispered the inquiry agent, as he remembered the name woven into the design. "Maggie Hemp." He tapped his boot. The mystery of Adelaide Harris was growing clearer.

For a long while there was silence in the little room during which Mr. Raven stared across the sea. Then he began to fumble in his pockets and bring out several folded pieces of paper. One by one he opened them and smoothed them out till he found one of a suitable size. Then he settled down to write with a pen that seemed to writhe and strike at the paper like a serpent.

He wrote names: Adelaide Harris, the gypsy baby, Mister Ralph, the Sorleys of Cuckfield, Maggie Hemp, Dr. Harris—and et cetera. He was not such a fool as to imagine he knew everything yet. There was always the et cetera—the dark spider who would be at the center of the web.

But they were all connected somehow; that much he did know. He smiled rather grimly to himself when he reflected how quickly he had involved the seemingly innocent Dr. Harris in the fine mesh of deceit. In view of this he was relieved he'd not taken luncheon with the Harrises. He would not have eaten with them now if they'd begged him on their bended knees.

For a moment he had been sorely tempted to put Dr. Harris's name in place of the unknown spider, the et cetera of the web; but an obscure sense bade him hold his pen. It was this quality that made him the formidable man he was and ever prevented him allowing personal resentment to cloud his pursuit of truth. After all, what did it matter that they hadn't asked him to lunch?

He left the central portion of his plan empty, folded the paper and replaced it in his pocket.

"No matter, they are all monsters, one way and another." He stood up, his face clouded with the anguish of triumph; there was always anguish in Mr. Raven's triumphs, for his was a nature that looked for goodness but found only the spots that rotted it away.

He rapped his boot. "Beside them, even you are a thing of beauty." Then he stumped out of the room and down the stairs in search of necessary fresh air.

As he left the Old Ship, the distant bell of St. Nicholas's chimed six o'clock and, shortly after, a baby began to howl; then another and another, till a thin, despairing anthem filled the fishy air. It came from the poorhouse: a tall, black building that lay behind the Old Ship Inn. The foundlings—of which at present there were five—were hungry. The inquiry agent nodded. "Howl," he whispered bitterly. "Howl your little agonies and curses—till you are grown enough to take your revenge on this vile world. And then in your turn suffer again."

Tap-thump . . . tap-thump . . . The inquiry agent passed under the high windows of the poorhouse. But now his ears were shut to the sad howling. He was brooding on another actor in the drama of which the disappearance of Adelaide Harris was but the first scene. There was still the man with the secret; the man who had ignored him so completely that even Mr. Raven's clubfoot had not been honored with a glance.

"Brett," muttered the inquiry agent. "What manner of a monster are you?"

Tap-thump . . . tap-thump . . .

# 9

A BOY APPEARED at the corner of the building; a burly boy, though looking quaintly small in a cut-down sea captain's coat that was still too large; a red-faced boy with fierce little eyes that Mr. Raven recognized as violent and savage.

Tap-thump . . . tap-thump . . . The boy stiffened and glared at the advancing inquiry agent. Terror, confusion and guilt were written all over him. Mr. Raven smiled; he was used to that. The boy licked his lips, glanced towards the poorhouse and whistled. Almost at once another boy appeared. This newcomer was somewhat stunted and malignant-looking. Mr. Raven knew him; he was the son of Dr. Harris.

"Good evening, my young friend," said Mr. Raven affably.

"Meet Bostock!" said Harris rapidly, and gave a little hysterical laugh. "My friend Bostock. Bosty, this is Mr. Selwyn Raven what I told you of." He thrust Bostock between himself and the man with the horrible boot.

So, thought the inquiry agent with weary contempt, you have been attempting to rob the poorhouse. Perhaps you've already done so? But no matter. Boys will be thieves . . . and then they'll be men and fouler still. But outwardly he maintained his look of affability. He was not a man to waste his time on little crimes. He preferred them to bloat and fatten before he pricked them to let the poison out. None the less he saw the boys were petrified with fear and guilt and would, most likely, oblige him with their grimy little souls if he kept their secret.

"Up to mischief?" he chuckled. "Well, well! Boys will be—he!—he!—boys! But I'll not say a word, my young friends! I too was a lad, once!" He thumped his boot with his stick. "Weren't we, eh?"

"That's very decent of you, sir," said Harris; and, to Bostock's undying admiration, gave a careless smile. Bostock knew it was a careless smile because it was quite different from Harris's ordinary smile. Harris was a real marvel; he, Bostock, was quite dried up with terror, having been warned of the clubfooted devil.

"Brett," said Mr. Raven abruptly, after talking idly about this and that, as was his habit to put the boys at their ease. "Do you know a man called Brett?"

Harris looked at him in utter astonishment. What on earth was Mr. Brett to do with anything? The inquiry agent, observing this astonishment, which was plainly genuine, felt a sudden pang at his heart. Whatever trifling crime the boy might be carrying on his soul, there was no doubt he was innocent of the terrible darkness that lay beneath the affair of Adelaide Harris. It moved the inquiry agent strangely to have stumbled on this little patch of innocence in the wide, crawling desert of sin.

"Mr. Brett's a master at our school—Dr. Bunnion's," said Harris; and another huge piece of the puzzle fell into place in Mr. Raven's mind. Another connection. The school. The innocent son of Dr. Harris . . . and Mr. Brett, et cetera, et cetera! Snap, snap, snap went the links of the chain; in his remarkable inner eye the inquiry agent saw all the actors in the drama like spectral dancers weaving across some ominous shoulder of the Downs, fettered to one another by lust, hatred, vengeance and greed, et cetera. But who was it who led the dance and dragged it on to his chosen perdition? Mr. Raven could hardly wait to get back to his room and embark on a larger piece of paper; but there was still more he needed to know. He had to be sure . . .

"Tell me about this Mr. Brett," said the inquiry agent gently. "What manner of—er—gentleman is he?"

At once Bostock and Harris obliged with all they knew and suspected of Mr. Brett. They talked very freely and eagerly, which amused Mr. Raven as he guessed it was to distract him from their private concerns. Though he was a sinister and even frightening man, he was also a man of honor. It was perhaps this that made him truly terrible; he could laugh with one part of his mind while the other continued to gather all those materials with which he built the vaults of human hell.

So he smiled and nodded while Bostock and Harris told him of Mr. Brett's pallors and tremblings at every knock on the door, his fearful looks when asked even about historical murders, his strange reluctance to leave the school for so much as an afternoon, and his most certain guilt of some unspeakable crime, most likely in the north.

When they were done, Mr. Raven thanked them gravely, flattered them by calling them his assistants, then tapped and thumped his grim way towards that tangled nest of cobbled alleys called by some The Twittens and, by others, The Lanes, where there was a shop that sold paper of the larger size.

Bostock and Harris, much shaken by the encounter, walked along beside the whispering sea.

"I think you got the better of him, Harris," said Bostock shrewdly.

Harris nodded. "But he's a clever man, Bosty. Don't underestimate him. That question about Mr. Brett was a real banger."

"Why's that, Harris?"

"Sparta, Bosty. If he'd got on to that talk of Mr. Brett's about Spartan infants being exposed, he'd have guessed and it would have been all up with us."

Bostock halted and whistled at the narrowness of their escape. Harris patted him on the shoulder. "One needs a long spoon to sup with gents like Mr. Raven."

They walked on again, picking their way round the drying fishing nets above which flies wove glinting puzzles in the stinking air. The failure of their recent attempt to rescue Adelaide from the poorhouse weighed heavily on the friends. They had been so very near to success. Harris had actually got into the room where the foundlings were kept. No one else had been there at that moment. The poorhouse keeper must have gone to the privy or something. It had been a remarkable piece of luck such as happened once in a lifetime. Harris had been laughing at the ease of it all.

"And there she lay, Bosty: my sister. Right at the end of the row. I think she knew me, Bosty. She gave a sort of smile. Just another minute and I'd have had her. Then you whistled . . ."

Bostock scowled and, picking up a stone, hurled it into the sea. "He was coming, Harris. I had to warn you."

Harris nodded. The friends halted and gazed mournfully back towards the poorhouse. They dared not return; yet it seemed unbearable not to.

"There's only one thing to do," said Harris at length.

"Own up?" said Bostock faintly. "Tell the truth?"

Harris looked at his friend with a universe of pity in his face. Bostock's simplicity touched him and made him feel curiously protective. He wondered how long Bostock would have survived in this stern world without his Harris.

"The truth?" he said gently. "What is truth, Bosty? There ain't no such thing, old friend. There's no truth in nature, Bosty; and that's where it counts. Everything has to hide to survive. Truth in the wild means sudden death; and truth at home ain't much better. And anyway," he added, "it's too late to own up now, old friend."

"What then, Harris?" whispered Bostock, another bastion of

his innocent young soul cracked and tottering from this last intellectual blow of his friend's.

"A letter, Bosty. An anonymous letter to my pa. It's the only way. A letter informing him where Adelaide really is. Then he can go and fetch her and no one will be any the wiser."

Bostock sighed. "You're a genius, Harris."

Then the friends shook hands and dispersed to their homes.

There was a quiet on the Harris household; there was an aimlessness, also, as if certain invisible threads that had held the family in order and regulation had been severed and so exposed the bleak loneliness of souls. Private chasms of fear had opened in every heart . . . and grinning calamity squatted in the hearth.

The Harris sisters were in the kitchen with the servants, picking at a vague dinner of cold mutton and cheese. Dr. Harris was out, and Mrs. Harris, the distraught mother, was crouching in the nursery where the strange baby still lay like a nightmare in Adelaide's cot.

Morgan, the nurse, was certain the infant was a changeling, an uncanny creature left by those malignant sprites who were the fallen angels of some ancient faith. There was no other explanation. She reminded Mrs. Harris that, against all advice, Adelaide had been christened in the goblin font of St. Nicholas's with its ugly pagan carvings grinning in the stone. Angrily Mrs. Harris had told her to hold her tongue, but Morgan, who was Celtic and wise in country ways, could not be silenced. She went on and on until Mrs. Harris had bowed her aching head and allowed Morgan to consult her elder sister who was even wiser.

So Morgan had gone off to call on the Hemps where her sister had once been nurse and was now the cook. Both the sisters had come from Aberystwyth as quite young girls in search of fortunes and husbands; but, having found neither, had settled in the Hemp and Harris households to which they'd brought a touch of Celtic magic.

The sisters talked long and hard over a glass of cordial and Morgan then returned, with a parcel of strong herbs, through the devious Lanes at about half past six. For a few uneasy moments she'd fancied she heard the sound of unequal footsteps—a tap-thump . . . tap-thump—as if she was being followed, but soon she outdistanced them and reached the Harris home with her wild garlic, coltsfoot and sheep's sorrel safely under her arm.

The changeling was asleep, but its face clearly lacked the smooth innocence of a mortal babe. There were shadows and creases across it that hinted of weird dreams and dark passions a-brewing; and its little mouth was shut in a line of cruel pink.

"I got 'em, ma'am," breathed Morgan; and Mrs. Harris raised her tear-stained face uncomprehendingly. So Morgan, seeing the poor lady was beyond clear thinking, laid a strong hand on her shoulder and set about making a fragile ring of herbs round the cot. This done, she opened wide the window and bade Mrs. Harris repeat after her the Celtic rune her sister had told her.

At first Mrs. Harris, who was a God-fearing woman, was quite repelled and would have nothing to do with it; but at length she was worn down and haltingly pronounced the eerie spell. Though she did not understand it, it was a call into the darkness of the lost faith—a command to the invisible goblins and demons whose ghostly bishops, on midsummer nights, crossed the moonlit lawns of those churches and abbeys that had usurped the ancient shrines.

The uncanny words demanded the presence of the bringers of the changeling.

As they died away, a breeze sprang up and billowed out the curtains; then the door blew open with a sharp sound. And Harris came in. There was a look of intolerable curiosity on his face.

"For God's sake, go away!" cried his unhappy mother. "Haven't I enough to bear?"

Harris stared in bewilderment at the circled herbs and silently withdrew.

"He's gone and spoiled it, ma'am," said Morgan bitterly. "Just like all else he sets his hand to."

For the remainder of the evening and several times during the night, Harris had a strong smell of herbs in his nostrils and an overwhelming desire to go again into the nursery; but the memory of the bitter words from Morgan and his mother rankled in his heart, and, with difficulty, he conquered the impulse. Instead, he lay awake and composed the anonymous letter he had determined to send to his father, the letter that would bring the whole terrific affair to a quiet and sensible conclusion.

Simple, brief and to the point. Bostock would write it. No one knew Bostock's writing; indeed, there were very few who knew Bostock could actually write. Bostock would write it during Monday's school, and it would be delivered on the same day; poked under the door at half after five. Harris sighed and smiled as he drifted on the tide of sleep. Why hadn't he thought of it before? Tomorrow . . . the poorhouse . . . Adelaide . . . home at last . . .

# 10

SORLEY, THE FAT BOARDER, driven half out of his mind by guilt on account of Mr. Brett following him everywhere, had at last come to terms with his conscience and taken a stolen veal pie out of concealment, scratched "Sorley is sorry, sir" on the crust, and placed it in Mr. Brett's bedroom. This done, he was able to pass into an untroubled sleep from which he awoke wretchedly hungry but spiritually refreshed.

Mr. Brett, on the other hand, awoke to considerable bewilderment and discomfort. He had not expected the pie—which Sorley had laid by the end of his bed—and had trodden in it. Thus all traces of its origin were obliterated and Mr. Brett was left, standing on one foot, much puzzled by the broken mystery.

At last he decided it must have come from Tizzy's mother, Mrs. Alexander. There was good reason for his supposing this as, for some time now, he had been giving Tizzy lessons in Classical History when school was over. Whether his passionate love for Mrs. Alexander's daughter had begun with the lessons or just before them, was no longer possible to say; but there was no doubt the lessons aggravated it. As he sat in the empty classroom, waiting for her gentle knock, his heart thundered so that he almost jumped out of his skin when at last it came.

It had been Mrs. Alexander herself who had suggested the

lessons—her German heart lifting to a scholar—and in return for improving her daughter—as if *I* could improve *her*, thought Mr. Brett with a sigh—she mended his linen and had promised to make him a shirt. "For your veddink, Herr Prett," she'd added with a sentimental smile. "Veneffer it shoot pe."

Mrs. Alexander's English had once been much better, but the longer she lived with her husband, the fiery Major, the further she retreated into the tongue of her childhood—as if striving to recapture the illusions she'd had when she'd never understood a word the Major said.

Mr. Brett sat on his bed, wiped his foot and smiled. He liked Mrs. Alexander and would have gone to thank her directly; but the damage done to the pie, he thought, would make him look awkward and ungrateful, so he waited till breakfast and contented himself with smiling meaningfully at her across the table whenever the occasion offered. At first Mrs. Alexander was frankly puzzled; but then she smiled back as if with a suddenly kindled optimism.

"You giff Tizzy her lesson today?" she murmured as they left the table. Mr. Brett nodded warmly. "Goot! Better than anythink, it takes her mind off this shtoopid business vit that Relph Bunnion."

"Very decent of you to take trouble with my gel," muttered the Major, brushing between his wife and Mr. Brett. "Improving a gel's mind is as good as giving her a rich dowry, I always say. Whoever gets her ought to be grateful to you, Brett. Take it as a personal favor. We don't say much, eh? But friendship between men . . . hoops of steel and all that."

The Major hurried away leaving Mr. Brett to gaze after him with a feeling of hopeless anger. Major Alexander always succeeded in infuriating him into silence. Friendship between men was not something that was uppermost in his thoughts; nor deeper down, neither. He frowned and went towards his classroom.

Major Alexander did not follow suit. Instead, by devious and almost underground ways, he went to Dr. Bunnion's study where he appeared with the somewhat quizzical air of a man gauging how much powder would be needed to bring down everything in sight. Dr. Bunnion looked at him uneasily. The Major compressed his lips and closed the door.

"My dear sir," he murmured, appearing to examine the walls, "a few minutes of your time is all I ask."

Dr. Bunnion nodded helplessly and the Major, having satisfied himself about the walls, fixed his eyes on the headmaster's desk. "Strictly speaking, sir, it's my—um—second's place to be here; but for good reasons—very good reasons, I might say—I've come myself. I'm not a bloodthirsty man. Your military men rarely are. It's your damned civilians who are always so keen on blood. What I want to say, sir, is that this unhappy affair is not of my choosing."

"The challenge was yours, Major Alexander," said Dr. Bunnion bitterly.

"No choice," said the Major. "My child's honor and all that; and a gel's honor, I need hardly tell you, is a delicate flower. Had to act as a father, you know. But now I've come to see you, man to man, to discuss what might be done about avoiding bloodshed. A parley, you might say, sir."

He laid his hands on Dr. Bunnion's desk and leaned forward, staring very confidentially at the headmaster's cravat. "To be open and aboveboard, sir, I'm fond of your boy. He's a fine fellow and I'd have been content to have him as a son-in-law. In a way, you might say that I love the lad as a son—and that's why I don't aim to stand in his way." Here the Major gave a little skip sideways, as if to illustrate his point. "I understand your ambitions for the lad. Good God! What father wouldn't? But there's me family's honor which is, and always will be, dearer to me than blessed life itself."

The Major gnawed his lip and, having finished with Dr. Bunnion's cravat, looked searchingly at his fingers. He leaned forward still further till the headmaster could make out the powder in the Major's military wig, and also a few cake crumbs. "But there is a compromise, sir," breathed the Major, and went on to mention that, in addition to his daughter, he had a son.

Dr. Bunnion laid his fingers together and pursed his lips. He knew of the Major's son—and of the Major's difficulties in finding a situation for him.

"I understand he's in a monastery," murmured the headmaster cautiously.

"It didn't suit," said the Major. "He—ha-ha—he couldn't acquire the habit! Truth of the matter is, he wants to teach. I think he's got a talent for it."

"But—" began Dr. Bunnion hopelessly.

"Brett," breathed the honorable Major. "No good, you know. Sly; secretive. I can't bear underhand men. If Brett goes, good thing for the school; then my boy Adam comes. Even better. What d'you say, sir?"

The Major skipped back and stared at the headmaster's waistcoat as if to divine what was going on within. In addition to being honorable, the Major was a reasonable man. Though he would have preferred to marry off Tizzy to Ralph, he was quite prepared to settle for the chance of planting his son Adam in the Bunnion stronghold and so increasing his grip on it. If the headmaster agreed, at one stroke the Major would have avoided the duel, ridded himself of the contemptible Brett, who, he always felt, looked down on him, and acted in the best interests of his family.

Dr. Bunnion was silent. As a father, the Major's offer appealed to him; but as a man he shrank from it. He did not at all like the idea of being outnumbered by the Alexanders in his own establishment, and he felt awkward about dismissing Mr. Brett who was, after all, acting as his son's second.

"Thought it best to have a word with you," said the Major, smiling cunningly at the headmaster's left ear and deciding to let his offer simmer for a day or so. "Man to man. Though we don't say much, deep down I fancy we understand each other. Real friendship . . . silent . . . strong . . . hoops of steel and all that. Settle it out of court, eh?"

Whereupon the Major withdrew and made his way towards his own classroom. He went by way of the kitchen as he thought it best, in everyone's interests, that he should not be seen coming from Dr. Bunnion's study. It was thus that he happened to see a maidservant gossiping at the side door with a stranger.

Inquisitively the Major halted. He peered over the maid's shoulder. The stranger had a pleasant, innocent-looking face; but he was burdened with a clubfoot.

"Yes," said the maid. "We do 'ave a Mr. Brett. Quiet gent, but a bit crafty if you ask me."

"Indeed, I do ask you," said the stranger gently. "What makes you think he is crafty?"

"He ain't as honest as he pretends," said the maid who had, that very morning, come upon the ruined veal pie in Mr. Brett's bedroom and recognized it as having been stolen from the larder.

At this point, Major Alexander, feeling that he could be more helpful about Mr. Brett, interposed with a curt "good morning," and proceeded to set the stranger to rights about Mr. Brett.

It really was a stroke of extraordinary good fortune. The Major guessed at once that the stranger was an inquiry agent out for Mr. Brett's blood. He'd had experience of such men before. Whatever Mr. Brett was suspected of, the Major had no idea, but he'd have laid odds on its being something pretty unpleasant. Thus he was able to look on the blackening of Mr. Brett's character as being in the way of a public duty. The Major was really a very scrupulous man. He prided himself on never having performed a mean or underhand act in his whole life without honor, duty or family love being mixed up in it somewhere. In the present instance he believed he could trace the presence of all three.

Mr. Raven listened gravely. What he'd heard fulfilled his hopes, but did not surprise him. But even yet he was cautious. There was nothing impetuous about the inquiry agent. He needed to make doubly and trebly sure before he could be committed to a course of action. He could not afford to be wrong. He took out a grubby pewter snuffbox and snapped it open, with the idea of distracting the Major into an unguarded admission.

"Hemp," he said quietly. "Does the name Hemp mean anything to you?"

As Mr. Raven had intended, the Major was momentarily nonplussed; then, becoming aware of the snuffbox which gave off a very sour smell, he was reminded of a campaign among the docks at Deptford, and a queer pipe of tobacco . . .

"D'you mean Indian hemp?"

"I would have thought more gypsy," said Mr. Raven carefully, as he thought of the baby in Adelaide Harris's cot.

"Could be," said the Major, thinking of the swarthy seaman who'd offered him the interesting smoke. "Or even Lascar. But gypsy or Lascar, they're all queer customers not to be trusted. I don't know much about them myself, of course."

"Oh, but I do," said Mr. Raven, thinking of the name embroidered on Ralph Bunnion's waistcoat: Maggie Hemp.

"But I'll tell you one thing," said the Major, anxious to return to the subject that interested him. "I'd trust a gypsy before Brett any day."

With that, he left the clubfooted stranger and continued to his classroom, resolving as he walked that he'd write directly to his son, bidding him come to Dr. Bunnion's where there would shortly be a vacancy.

"Brett," muttered Mr. Raven as he clumped away from the school. "As we thought . . . the Prime Mover . . . Brett." Here the inquiry agent brushed so near to the truth of the Adelaide affair that the very angels in heaven spread their wings and prepared to flee.

"And Hemp with the gypsy blood . . . But Brett is the one. What is his real name? De Brett? Viscount Brett?" Mr. Raven preferred to look in high places for his corruption. The nobler the structure, the louder the uproar when he brought it tumbling down.

Tap-thump . . . tap-thump . . . He passed along the morning streets where women avoided him and fishermen spat. There was a briskish breeze coming off the sea and the distant waves wore scabs of white. The inquiry agent halted and stared across the water.

A strange exultation filled him as he sensed how close he was to understanding all parts of the mystery. So intricate was it that the smallest movement of each thread set up shiverings across the whole unsavory web. Only the previous evening he had observed Morgan, the Harris nurse, visiting the Hemps and hurrying guiltily away. Thus the connection between the two households had been confirmed and noted down. But who had sent her and on what desperate errand?

The inquiry agent scowled and shook his head. He suspected the affair was approaching some sinister climax. Perhaps his own presence was the cause? He walked on, much troubled by certain tiny aspects of the affair that still eluded him.

He was by the poorhouse and the morning wailing of the five foundlings mingled with the harsh laughter of the swooping seabirds. He leaned in the narrow shadow of the poorhouse wall, seeming to listen intently to the wordless misery the seagulls jeered at. Then, as if making a certain decision, he rapped his boot and clumped off out of the sunshine into the dark parlor of the Old Ship.

He settled himself in a corner, called for brandy and water, and then, making sure he was the only customer, took out a piece of paper from his pocket that unfolded almost to the size of the table top. "Brett," he whispered, studying the extraordinary design that reached now to the paper's edge, "the next move is yours, my friend." He turned the paper round. "What will it be, eh? No matter . . . no matter . . . we will be watching. And then, my friend, we will strike with a thunderbolt, et cetera."

While the inquiry agent was so engaged, his great adversary— Mr. Brett—was struggling with Ancient History in his classroom at the Academy. Fiercely he tried to pull over his head the paper layers of time and escape from everything. But wherever he turned in the Ancient World he seemed to be confronted by images of his own plight—encircling enemies and hopeless love.

In the back parlor, Major Alexander, though he now had every hope that the duel would not take place, was none the less uneasy that something might go wrong and he found himself setting his pupils terrific problems concerning the speed of bullets and the cost of coffins in English shillings and German marks.

Not even Dr. Bunnion himself was able to escape the shadowy fears that beset the school. As it was close to the end of term, the headmaster had planned to describe the building of Solomon's temple, right down to the last half cubit of an ornamental angel's wing, so that any boy, with skill and industry, might construct it for himself during the holiday. Instead the troubled father found himself brooding aloud on the sacrifice of Isaac. In his mind's eye he saw himself as Abraham, poised above the sacrifical stone on which lay the hapless Ralph. "And the angel of the Lord called unto him out of heaven . . . lay not thy hand upon the lad." And the angel spoke in the secret, clipped voice of Major Alexander. "And Abraham lifted up his eyes, and looked, and behold, behind him a ram caught in a thicket by its horns . . ." And the ram had the gentle, long-suffering face of Mr. Brett. "And Abraham went and took the ram and offered it up . . . instead of Ralph."

The class looked up in surprise; and Dr. Bunnion flushed and corrected himself. But the notion of sacrificing Mr. Brett to Major Alexander's honor gathered strength in his mind and tormented him throughout the day.

Just before luncheon, being unable to bear the weight of the problem any longer, he confided in Mrs. Bunnion who looked at him in amazement. To her there was no problem at all. He must close with the Major's offer and get rid of Mr. Brett directly. What right had Dr. Bunnion even to think of keeping Mr. Brett and so endangering Ralph's life? She had never heard of anything like it in all her born days! He was to stop behaving like a weakling and send Mr. Brett packing at once! Really! Who was he afraid of?

Mutely Dr. Bunnion gazed at his dignified wife who, though not as tall as he, morally overtopped him by a good six inches. So after the meal he made several attempts to corner Mr. Brett and at last succeeded in catching him at the foot of the stairs.

"Well?" began Dr. Bunnion harshly, seeking an opportunity of losing his temper and so dismissing Mr. Brett in hot rather than cold blood. "I suppose you haven't bothered to see Major Alexander's second?"

Mr. Brett nodded uneasily. He had. Dr. Bunnion looked taken aback. "What then? What did he say?"

"Saturday," said Mr. Brett. "In the morning."

"But that's the end of term! Good God! Couldn't he have waited till the holiday?" The headmaster stared at Mr. Brett in horror. "What an idea! Don't you know the parents will be here? What d'you imagine they'll think when they find my son bleeding to death—perhaps already dead—and my Arithmetic master in jail for it? What kind of a school d'you suppose they'll think I conduct? Saturday! You must be mad, Brett—"

"But it wasn't up to me, sir—"

"Couldn't you have explained to Alexander's second? It was your duty!"

Feebly Mr. Brett shook his head.

"Saturday!" repeated Dr. Bunnion savagely. "I'll tell you one thing, Brett"—at last he felt his blood to be heated enough to obey Mrs. Bunnion—"before Saturday comes you'd—"

"—Sorley!" cried Mr. Brett, seeing the fat boarder pass by. "Come here, boy!" He reached out and clutched him by the shoulder, then turned back to Dr. Bunnion in desperate triumph. "I—I interrupted you, sir."

"You'd better—er—see about Dr. Harris," muttered the headmaster, thwarted by the presence of the baronet's son. Then he shambled away, his blood cooling in defeat.

Mr. Brett, still holding on to Sorley, gazed after him. How much longer could he hope to survive in this dangerous world? Till Saturday, perhaps? "Come, boy," he whispered. "Soon it will be Saturday . . . and the end."

He walked slowly to his classroom together with the fat boarder who kept staring up at him piteously. But Mr. Brett had no eyes for Sorley. He was thinking of Tizzy Alexander and how soon he was fated to leave her. The look on Dr. Bunnion's face had been unmistakable. His time was running out. His days in the school were numbered; and the headmaster had decided on what the number was to be. His last chance had come. He would have to tell Tizzy he loved her—or resign himself to never seeing her again.

His eyes filled with tears at the very thought of living without her. He would risk all and tell her that very afternoon. Good God! He was a grown man—not a tongue-tied lovesick child! And if he kept silent he'd lose her for certain. James Brett, you fool—take her firmly in your arms, look into her eyes and say, after me, "I love you, Tizzy Alexander; with all my heart and soul, I love you, my dear . . ."

These thoughts so filled his imagination that the afternoon lesson went by as in a dream. His twelve pupils threw ink pellets, tormented Sorley and buzzed and hovered from place to place; but they troubled him no more than the antics of the classroom flies.

It was during this time that Bostock, under Harris's anxious guidance, wrote the letter that was to inform Dr. Harris, anonymously, of the whereabouts of his lost daughter, Adelaide. He'd had several attempts at it that, for one reason and another, had been abandoned, but eventually it was completed almost to Harris's satisfaction. Afterwards, Mr. Brett remembered vaguely having seen Bostock writing something with Harris, his evil genius, bending over him. But he'd had too much on his mind to be more than remotely curious; and in a little while the memory faded altogether.

"Just think of it, Bosty," said Harris cheerfully as the friends walked home. "Tonight we'll have Adelaide back again."

# II

THE INQUIRY AGENT, despite his immensely active mind, was a man of great patience. Though this quality had at first been imposed on him by his deformity—which prevented rapid movement—he had cultivated it until it had become perhaps his most formidable attribute. He could wait a lifetime, if necessary, to trap and destroy his prey. But when at last he moved, the unhurried tap-thump of his stick and boot was as relentless and terrible as the approach of the angel of death.

He sat in the back parlor of the Old Ship awaiting word of the move he knew must come. The only other occupant of the parlor was Ralph Bunnion's friend, Frederick. From time to time Frederick glanced at him with nervous amiability; Mr. Raven fingered his glass and smiled deprecatingly at his boot.

"Poor bastard!" muttered Frederick impulsively. At bottom he was a generous and even kindly young man. Mr. Raven looked up and Frederick reddened and hid his face in his tankard.

"Indeed, you're right!" said Mr. Raven eagerly moving closer. "I *am* very narrow in my means—and certainly might be considered poor next to you and your friends. And, as for the other, there's no doubt about it. I was a foundling, you know. But it's all God's will, young man. He knows best."

"I—I—" began Frederick, then breathed a sigh of relief when he saw Ralph Bunnion enter the parlor. But the damage had been done. Having been neatly trapped into extending sympathy to the man with the clubfoot, he could not get rid of him when Ralph came to sit down. Not that the horrible fellow seemed to push himself forward; it was just that he wouldn't move away. He sat, too close for comfort, meekly silent and staring at his boot in the most pathetic manner imaginable.

"Saturday," muttered Ralph at length, seeing further privacy was impossible. "It's to be Saturday. Brett told my pa yesterday; so you'd better get the you-know-whats oiled and ready."

"I've got 'em here, old dear," breathed Frederick, producing the case of pistols and endeavoring to conceal them from the clubfooted man's innocent eyes.

"Not now. Saturday, I said."

"Where?"

The stranger bent forward with involuntary interest. Frederick stared at him with hostility. An unwise expression; Mr. Raven made a mental note to enmesh him in the design. The inquiry agent was a dangerous man to cross.

"Brett will tell you," said Ralph.

"Brett—Brett!" exclaimed Frederick peevishly. He was hurt and angry that Mr. Brett seemed to be supplanting him in an affair where he, of all people, should be standing closest to Ralph. After all, he was Ralph's friend, and he was providing the pistols. "It's always Brett these days, ain't it! Anybody would think he'd arranged the whole thing!"

"They would indeed," breathed Mr. Raven, finishing his drink and heaving himself upright. "They would indeed, my friend." He nodded politely to the two young men and clumped out of the parlor to make certain additions to the architecture of his plan.

The Harris household had spent a grim day. Mrs. Harris could not be persuaded to leave the nursery and Dr. Harris had given instructions that she was not to be left alone there for more than a few minutes. Her grief had shown no signs of diminishing and the doctor had very real fears that she would do the mysterious gypsy baby an injury.

Even when the wet nurse came to perform her duty, it was only under the haggard eyes of the forlorn mother and, as she confided in Morgan the nurse, "It's a wonder me milk don't curdle into cheese."

The wet nurse came in the afternoons at about a quarter after five. Dr. Harris himself let her in and took her upstairs; he was a humane man and did not want the unknown baby to suffer. Thus when there came a knock on the door at the expected time, the doctor was rather put out to find that it was Mr. Brett from the school, wanting a word with him.

"I'd be obliged if you'd be brief, Mr. Brett," he said, remaining in the hall. "As you must know, we have great family troubles . . ."

Mr. Brett nodded. He didn't know, but on the other hand he had enough troubles of his own without being burdened with Dr. Harris's.

"Dr. Bunnion would be grateful, sir," he said, coming directly to the point, "if you would attend a duel on Saturday morning."

Dr. Harris gaped at him; and Mr. Brett explained matters as briefly and discreetly as he could. The doctor sighed and shrugged his shoulders. At any other time he would have been amazed and fascinated; but the loss of Adelaide so dominated his mind that all else seemed trifling. "You understand that I am a physician, Mr. Brett; not a surgeon—"

"But Dr. Bunnion was particularly anxious, sir—"

At this point Dr. Harris heard the unmistakable shuffle and flop of the wet nurse's step. "Very well—very well," he muttered agitatedly. "Let me know the time and place. Now, if you please, good day to you, sir." He opened the door to let Mr. Brett out and the wet nurse in. "Duels—duels," he grunted. "Has all the world gone mad?"

Mr. Brett, who had expected all manner of difficulties to be put in his way and had been fully prepared for failure and the consequent anger of Dr. Bunnion, could not help smiling with happy triumph at the ease of his success. It gave him unexpected confidence in himself and made him think that perhaps he possessed a more powerful personality than he'd supposed. He broke into a brisk trot as he made his way back to the school and his beloved Tizzy.

The world was suddenly a beautiful place and he seemed as light as the bright warm air. Seagulls flew like angels above him and he looked upward as if he was on the point of soaring among them. He did not see the man with the clubfoot who happened to be standing at the corner of the street.

"It is beginning," muttered the inquiry agent, grimly noting Mr. Brett's rapid pace and triumphant smile. "The end is beginning. When the Devil runs, can Hell be far away?"

There was a coolness between Bostock and Harris. The delivering of the anonymous letter was partly to blame; the rest was on account of a bouquet of wildflowers Bostock wanted to give to Mary Harris, whom he particularly admired, as it was her birthday.

"Give 'em to her tomorrow," Harris had said impatiently. "Another day won't signify." He did not want Bostock, who was ink-stained from writing the anonymous letter, appearing at his house on the same day as the letter itself.

"They'll have faded," said Bostock obstinately.

"Who cares?" said Harris with more than a touch of irritation; then, seeing that Bostock looked offended, he instantly regretted his tone. He sensed that his friend was affected by that soft passion that he, Harris, knew to be as disrupting as it was unscientific. He smiled at his scowling friend who was grasping the bouquet like a weapon.

"I know how you feel, Bosty," he murmured kindly. "You fancy you're in love with Mary."

Bostock reddened; Harris was uncanny.

"But I'm afraid there's no such thing as what you call love, old friend."

Bostock braced himself, and Harris continued. "It's only an instinct, old friend; nothing more than that. It's like—like blowing your nose; you have to do it, and you feel better when you've done it."

Bostock stared mournfully at the bouquet he had so laboriously gathered. If Harris was right—and he always was—he should have got Mary a pocket handkerchief.

"We all have these instincts, Bosty," went on Harris. "Generally we get them when we're thirteen or thereabouts. I'll be getting them myself, any day now. You see a female and right away you want to have carnal knowledge of her."

"Carnal knowledge?"

"Poke her," explained Harris. "It's the law of nature, Bosty."

Bostock thought of the wild, slender Miss Harris—and blushed to the roots of his soul. He looked down at the little forest all jeweled with tiny blossoms that he was clutching. "Is that really all it is, Harris?" he asked sadly.

"That's all, Bosty," said Harris compassionately; and, to his relief, Bostock let the flowers fall. Who'd have thought Mary would so nearly have come between them?

"Five minutes after six, Bosty," went on Harris after a pause to allow his friend to bring his mind to the matter in hand. "That's the time to do it. Poke—er—push the letter under the door and then go like the wind."

Bostock nodded and Harris held out his hand. Bostock hesitated.

"Old friend," said Harris. "It all depends on you." Bostock sighed and the friends shook hands.

Harris made a good deal of noise as he entered his house so that the time of his arrival should be generally known and not confused with the arrival of the letter. He went up to the nursery and engaged the wet nurse in conversation while she, poor soul, all but suffocated the black-haired baby under her shawl as she modestly tried to hide her breast from Harris's inquisitive gaze.

At five minutes after six Harris's heart began to beat violently. The time had come. He strained his ears, but he heard nothing. Bostock must have been as silent as the air.

"Well, that's all for now, you gutsy little darlin'," said the wet nurse, returning the baby to its cot and her breast to her gown. She nodded to Morgan and went downstairs. Harris followed her. He stared towards the front door. There was no letter. Dismay seized Harris. Had Bostock deserted him? After all he'd said, had love really deprived him of his friend?

The wet nurse shuffled down the last stairs—when something white flew from under the door with tremendous force and vanished under the wet nurse's skirts. It had been the letter. Bostock, ever faithful to his friend, had kept his word; but resentment at the shattering of yet another illusion had caused him to be overstrong.

Dr. Harris, hearing the wet nurse in the hall, came out of his study to pay her. Harris the younger glared at the ragged hem of her gown. She took the money, lifted her dress to stow it away in her petticoat—and saw the letter.

She picked it up and gave it to the doctor. "It's yours, sir," she said and, jingling slightly, she shuffled out of the house.

Dr. Harris opened the letter and read it. Harris watched his father's face in an agony of expectation which, however, he concealed under a mild interest.

"W—what is it, Pa? Anything . . . important?"

The doctor frowned. "The impudence of it! Sending that wretched woman with their begging letters! Don't I do enough for charity as it is?" Wearily he showed his son the paper on which Bostock, after so many attempts, had at last revealed the whereabouts of Adelaide. "Dear Dr. Harris," he had written. "Think of the poorhouse."

The doctor fumbled in his pockets. "Here, son," he said. "Take this down to the poorhouse with my compliments."

He gave the dazed Harris a handful of silver, crumpled up the letter and trudged upstairs to the nursery. Harris stared after him in an agony of rage and disbelief. There were tears in his eyes. Everything seemed against him; even his own father . . .

He left the house and slammed the door behind him as if he would shake his home to the ground. Though Bostock was ever a great comfort to him, he was glad that his friend was not at his side. Harris doubted whether he could have restrained himself from blaming Bostock for the horrible failure of the scheme. Bostock had pushed the letter so unnecessarily hard that if the back door had been open it would most likely have gone clean through the house. There was no doubt that everything now rested on Harris's shoulders; and he felt they were cracking.

Bitterly he counted up the money his distraught father had given him: nineteen shillings. In the old days, such a sum would have filled him with wonderment and joy. But now it weighed him down. He walked on towards the poorhouse while the sun, sinking in an irony of crimson, orange and gold, served only to deepen the private night of his despair.

He would have to give the money to the poorhouse. His father might meet Mr. Bonney, the keeper, at any time and mention it. But on the other hand, so large a sum as nineteen shillings would be sure to startle Mr. Bonney into mentioning it of his own accord. Then the affair of the letter would be bound to come out; and then everything else.

Harris moaned. Then he frowned; then he half-smiled. Why hand over all the nineteen shillings? What was wrong with five? He paused and completed his smile. He rubbed his hands together. Mr. Bonney would accept five shillings gratefully and not think twice about it, Harris nodded shrewdly. All problems, however great, yielded to a little thought. Five from nineteen left fourteen shillings. A handsome sum. Harris brooded. Quite by chance he seemed to have hit on a remarkable way of making money. When the affair of Adelaide was cleared up, he and Bostock might work on a grander scale . . .

"Good evening, my young friend."

Harris almost jumped out of his skin. The hateful Mr. Raven, who had been taking the evening air outside the Old Ship, suddenly accosted him.

"I didn't mean to startle you," said the inquiry agent apologetically. "You must have been quite lost in thoughts. Were I a rich man, ha-ha! I'd offer you a penny for them."

Harris smiled feebly.

"Come, let me guess. A young lady perhaps?" Mr. Raven gazed slyly down at his boot. "Are you on your way to a tryst?"

Harris laughed lightly. "Just to the poorhouse, sir. My pa asked me to give them some charity money." Harris was honest enough to be truthful when he didn't see that it could do any harm. "A very charitable man, my pa."

"Very," agreed Mr. Raven, and waved the boy on his way. He watched him disappear into the poorhouse, then shook his head and returned to the frontage of the Old Ship where he set about wondering if there was a space left for the poorhouse keeper in the frightful web of which Mr. Brett was the center and Adelaide Harris no more than a single, unimportant thread.

After a few minutes the brilliance of the setting sun reflecting on the sea distracted him and irritated his sensitive eyes; so he went to take his brandy and water in the gloom of the back parlor. His heart was heavy; the more he considered the complexity of the affair he was engaged upon, the more depressed and disgusted he became with the vileness of mankind.

Mr. Bonney, the poorhouse keeper, was away, but his wife, who liked to be called the matron, greeted Harris in his stead. "A real Christian," she said as she pocketed the five shillings Harris gave her. "No matter what 'is domination may be, I call 'im a real Christian and I'll say so to 'is face. And you're a little one, Master H. God bless you—on be'alf of our five 'ungry mouths."

Harris, after vainly peering over Mrs. Bonney's high shoulder for a sight of Adelaide, bowed and withdrew. On the dark, narrow stairs, he passed the wet nurse who, smelling of gin, was on her way to do her duty by the foundlings. She looked at Harris sharply, shrugged her sturdy shoulders and continued on her way, leaving Harris to meditate on the irony of the same milk feeding both Adelaide and the alien baby in her place.

Upstairs, Mrs. Bonney waited for the wet nurse to settle herself down before going across to the Old Ship. Five shillings was a largish sum to hand over to her husband without subtraction. Two and sixpence would be more than enough . . . and very nice too for the poor little mites. Which left a further two shillings and sixpence for brandy which was altogether healthier and more genteel than gin.

"Evening, Mrs. Bonney," said the landlord affably. "And how's them sinful brats of your'n?"

"It ill be'oves a publican to talk of sin," said Mrs. Bonney with dignity. "A large brandy, if you please; and a half of gin to cool it down."

The landlord smiled. He was too sensible a man to take offense at anything save a bad debt. He dispensed Mrs. Bonney's brandy and gin and took her money.

"From the charity bag, ma'am?" he murmured with a good-natured wink. "Ah well, them poor mites wouldn't have much use for strong waters, eh?"

"A decent Christian," said Mrs. Bonney, tasting her brandy, "don't mock the unfortunates of this world." Then she settled down and was much surprised and gratified to find herself admired by a gentle-looking stranger who suffered from the inconvenience of a clubfoot.

"You look after the poorhouse, ma'am?"

Mrs. Bonney nodded. "In a manner of speaking. I'm the matron."

"Godly work," said Mr. Raven.

"A vessel of charity," said Mrs. Bonney, cooling her brandy with a mouthful of gin.

"Charity," said Mr. Raven wistfully. "How little there is in the world."

"Oh, I don't know," said Mrs. Bonney thoughtfully. "It comes and goes."

"Now that lad I saw calling on you just now—Master Harris, wasn't it?" said Mr. Raven earnestly. "Do you often receive charity from the young?"

Mrs. Bonney looked at him sharply. "That were from 'is pa, sir," she said carefully. "And it were private. For Mr. Bonney. Nothing to do with charity." She had no intention of letting the stranger imagine she spent charity money on herself. She had a position to keep up. Being matron, she felt she ought to be above suspicion.

"A private—er—donation, then?" murmured the inquiry agent, almost to himself.

"Call it what you like," said Mrs. Bonney, becoming suddenly aloof. "It were something between Mr. Bonney and Dr. H. of which I am totally ignorant as God is my witness."

"Indeed, indeed," said Mr. Raven and gave such a smile that Mrs. Bonney was chilled to the bone and wondered who or what she had betrayed. "Pray to God it ain't you, Mr. Bonney," she whispered. She did not know that in her aloofness she had betrayed not her husband but herself. A space had just been found for her . . .

# 12

ONCE AGAIN MR. BRETT had failed to tell Tizzy Alexander that he loved her madly and could not see his way clear to living without her. He had arrived back at the school from his successful visit to Dr. Harris still full of confidence in his powers, to discover that Tizzy had been waiting in the empty classroom for all of fifteen minutes. His mood being high and feeling his personality to be equal to anything, he'd put on an air of negligent gallantry and made a joke of his lateness. Unluckily Tizzy, who was somewhat on edge on account of the coming duel and her own responsibility for it, had not thought it funny to have been kept waiting and so was distinctly cool. Whereupon Mr. Brett made a further error of judgment by attempting to explain, a shade too carefully, what had kept him.

"It is of no importance," she'd said, not listening. "I understand quite well that many matters must come before me. You don't have to find excuses, sir. It's perfectly all right with me if you choose to meet someone else in the town. These things happen, you know. Only I abhor excuses . . . so please don't trouble yourself. After all, when all's said and done, I know I'm only the Arithmetic master's daughter!"

With that she'd opened her book, fixed her shining eyes upon it—and Mr. Brett's soaring spirits had dipped. The words of love he'd so dearly prepared were once again wrapped up and put away in his heart's bottom drawer for some more propitious occasion. He fixed his mind on Ancient History and tried to sail off into that golden time; but something warned him that Tizzy was in a different boat, so to speak, and, from time to time, pupil and master glanced at each other with sad, puzzled eyes.

After the lesson he left the classroom in a mood of angry gloom—and collided with Major Alexander at whom he stared with absentminded savagery.

"To me son," mumbled the Major awkwardly. He was holding a letter and was sure Mr. Brett had seen it and read the address. It was the very letter in which the arrangements for Mr. Brett's dismissal were mentioned and the Major's son invited to hasten to fill his place. Consequently the Major was particularly anxious not to invite interest by appearing too furtive about it. "Setting me affairs in order, y'know," he explained, staring uneasily at Mr. Brett's clenched fists. "Saturday. If I should fall, and all that . . . Sentimental nonsense, of course; but one never knows. Last farewells, eh?"

"Yes . . . yes . . . Saturday," muttered Mr. Brett, and hurried on his way.

For several moments the Major remained, staring after him. He had never seen Mr. Brett look so angry and he could not help wondering if somehow he'd got an inkling of the private discussion with Dr. Bunnion.

He shook his head. He didn't see how that was possible. If Brett had really suspected anything, the Major felt sure that he'd have been rude enough to have mentioned it. The trouble was, the Major was too sensitive a man. People didn't realize how easily their chance expressions affected him; and he had so large a conscience that there was always something on it.

For the sake of his peace of mind he decided to postpone the sending of the letter until the following morning. He kept it under his pillow for the night. Next morning, after breakfast, he handed it, firmly sealed, to his wife for prompt dispatch.

Mrs. Alexander, large, fair and sad, read her husband's letter with a sigh that stretched from first word to last. Then she replaced the seal with a spot of melted tallow—an accomplishment she had come by in her years with the Major—and called for Tizzy to take the letter down to the town for the post.

When her daughter had gone Mrs. Alexander frowned and her eyes glimmered with tears. So, she thought bitterly, it's all arranged. Herr Brett is to go—and Adam is to come. What an exchange! And so soon! On Saturday, even. She blinked, then straightened her ample shoulders and went into Tizzy's room where, with rapid hands, she set about rummaging the shifts and petticoats to see what needed mending . . .

Tizzy, brightly pretty in her yellow spotted muslin and flower-embroidered cap, went down into the town like a butterfly. There was always a coachman or two in the yard of the Old Ship who'd carry a letter to Southwark to oblige a girl like Tizzy.

It was now nearly a month since Adam Alexander had been waiting at Southwark after leaving the monastery at Basingstoke at the abbot's request. "Burn me!" had shouted the Major's son, passionate for martyrdom, for the young man was something of a fire-brand, having inherited his father's temperament. "Why don't you burn me at the stake, then?" To which the abbot had wearily replied, "I'd be glad to, young man—but I rather fancy you're too wet to make a worthwhile blaze." So Adam had shaken his fist at the abbot and the dust of the cloisters from his sandaled feet and made his way to Southwark where he languished till his father should find him another situation.

Tizzy handed the letter to an ancient coachman and rewarded him with a shilling and a smile in place of the kiss he'd asked. Then, with the smile still about her—for to be asked for a kiss is a marvelous curver of the lips—she left the yard in time to meet with Ralph Bunnion who was on his way into the Old Ship's back parlor.

Aroused by Tizzy's beauty and tortured by the memory of what it had brought him to, Ralph halted. "It's all your fault!" he snarled. "When blood flows on Saturday, it'll be on your conscience forever! I hope you're satisfied." Then he said, "Murderess!" and stalked into the inn in a blaze of peach velvet and a flash of love-in-idleness.

Tizzy stared after him, her eyes stinging with tears at the injustice of it all. For a moment she wished with all her heart that Ralph Bunnion would indeed be slain on Saturday; but she repented instantly as that would have made her father a murderer. So did she wish her father killed instead? Again she recoiled from the thought. She began to walk away with downcast eyes and the ancient coachman who'd asked her for a kiss gazed after her and fancied she was limping, as if she'd stumbled and been bruised against one of the world's sharp corners.

"Charming young woman," murmured a stranger with a clubfoot.

"A lass and a half," agreed the coachman. "Sweet as a lane in May."

The inquiry agent smiled. Quite reasonably he had taken Tizzy to be Maggie Hemp as there seemed no purpose in introducing a newcomer to the scheme at this late stage. The threat of blood on Saturday and the terrible taunt of "Murderess" had further confirmed him. Cautiously he craned his neck to read the name on the letter the coachman still held. "Adam Alexander." Mr. Raven's brain reeled. Was there no end to the complexity of the affair? Were its hideous tentacles reaching out to yet another victim?

Every impulse bade him follow the young woman in the yellow dress; but his foot ached from the constant dragging from place to place. He groaned with frustration and heaved himself up to his little room where he spread out his paper and, in a few minutes, was calmed by studying it.

Blood on Saturday. At least he had until then. Everything indicated that Brett would hold his hand until that fatal day. "But on Saturday," he whispered to his boot, "we will forestall him and strike with a thunderbolt!"

Tizzy Alexander, after thinking miserably about casting herself from the top of Black Rock and so ending her young life on a romantic full stop, had decided to give the world just one more chance and had arrived back at the school before lunch. As she passed slowly before the front parlor window, she heard Mr. Brett talking about the infant Perseus being abandoned to the sea in a fragile ark. Strange how often babies seemed to be abandoned in the Ancient World as well as the modern. Dreamily, for Mr. Brett's voice always made her deliciously dreamy, she caught herself remembering the little baby she'd found on the Downs on that hateful afternoon when everything had begun. Between her other troubles, she'd thought of it often since it had been whisked away in Ralph Bunnion's lumpish arms. She'd wondered what had become of it and whether it was now being as loved as she'd have loved it if she'd been given the chance. Now she wondered how it would have been—with the baby of course—how it would have been if she'd gone walking with Mr. Brett instead of Ralph Bunnion. She remembered the last lesson—and sighed. He'd have talked of Ancient History all the way there and all the way back.

She peered through the window at the twelve large, clumsy boys who sprawled and huddled in their places like heaps of old clothes. It won't be long before they're lovers and husbands, she thought with amazement; even those two awful ones in the front . . . what were their names, now? Bostock and Harris. Her gaze shifted. And there's that poor, fat child, Sorley. But he looks so pale; and thinner. I must mention it to Ma. Perhaps he needs some physic?

She stopped. One by one the boys had turned and were staring at her. They were grinning. Alarmed, she looked to the front of the class. Mr. Brett was also staring at her. His eyes were enormous and his face was pale as death. He half raised a hand towards her—when she went as red as a poppy and fled into the school.

"Vy must you frighten the vits out of me, child?" said Mrs. Alexander angrily as Tizzy burst in upon her. "A leddy shoot knock." Then she shoveled away a large piece of white material into her workbox and shut the lid on it as if it were alive. Tizzy frowned.

As always, Bostock and Harris walked home together. The coolness between them had gone; theirs was a friendship that was strengthened by disaster. It was now as firm as a rock. Harris had confided in Bostock the misfortune that had overtaken the anonymous letter and had been generous enough not to blame his friend for it. Bostock had listened, staring at Harris in mute and terrified sympathy. He had never known Harris to fail in anything so many times. Bostock felt that it was fate; but he didn't like to say so as he knew Harris didn't believe in fate. None the less, there seemed no other explanation and Bostock, in his heart of hearts, was sure that Harris and he were opposed by a power that was beyond them. Genius though Harris undoubtedly was, there were still things in heaven and earth that even a genius might not overcome. He stole a mournful glance at Harris and wondered how he might tell him that it looked like Adelaide was gone for good.

But he couldn't bring himself to do it. He saw that Harris was battling with a new idea. Truly there was something heroic about Harris. In the face of all calamity, he fought indomitably on.

"There's fourteen shillings left," said Harris, brooding as if over a great distance. "And fourteen shillings could go a long way."

Bostock nodded and wondered how far Harris was considering going with it.

"Now if we was to invest it, little by little, in that Mrs. Bonney at the poorhouse . . ."

"Yes, Harris?"

The lights were beginning to flicker in Harris's eyes and, in spite of himself, Bostock couldn't help being excited.

"If we was to go each day with a shilling or two for the foundlings . . ."

"Yes, Harris?"

"So that our comings and goings would seem natural and aboveboard . . ."

He paused and looked inquiringly at Bostock for another "Yes, Harris," which somehow he seemed to need. "Then sooner or later she won't be there, Bosty. It happened before and it'll happen again."

"Yes, Harris?"

"So we lift Adelaide, Bosty, old friend! Easy as kiss your hand! Don't you see? It's as good as done! A little patience, a little money—and it'll all be over!"

Once more the lights were fully on in Harris's eyes. He was all triumph.

"And—even if it don't work again," said Bostock, striving to prepare his friend for the inevitable worst, "we'll have done a real charity with all that money for the foundlings!"

"Charity?" said Harris mockingly. "What's that, Bosty? My poor old friend, there ain't no such thing as charity." He laughed sardonically and Bostock steadied himself to have yet another support of his youthful soul knocked away.

"Hypocrisy," said Harris. "Nothing more, Bosty. Self-interest rules us all. The man what gives to the poor is only doing it to be well thought of by the world."

"But what about them that give secretly, Harris?"

"Worst of all," said Harris contemptuously. "They're the ones that spill it all out in their prayers to buy themselves a seat in Heaven. Sniveling in their pews: Look God, haven't I been good today? You'll remember, won't you, when the time comes?"

"But you said there wasn't any God—"

"Then more fool them and it serves them right when they find out they've done it all for nothing. No, Bosty, old friend—all your saints and philanthropists only give to satisfy themselves, else they wouldn't do it. Stands to reason. Hypocrites, every last one of 'em. Charity's a snare and a delusion, Bosty."

"But it's supposed to be Christian, anyway."

"What's that, Bosty? Mark my words, old friend, if there was such a thing as a real live Christian—which there can't be as nature's against it—he'd be honest enough and truthful enough in his own heart never to sink to your sneaking charity. He'd be a man, no matter how many poor he came across, no matter how they yelped and whimpered for bread, who'd not demean himself by giving anything away. He'd be a man who'd scorn to puff himself up with goodness. That's what I'd call a real Christian, Bosty! None of your sniveling hypocrites!'

Bostock stared at the ground. He was thinking of the shilling he'd put in the collecting box on Sunday; and he was deeply ashamed.


Mrs. Bonney, having drunk away the two shillings and sixpence of yesterday, was feeling the effects of it. Mr. Bonney was still away so she still had the remaining money and she was sorely tempted. The stranger with the clubfoot had put the fear of the Devil into her—else she'd never have drunk so freely. Now her temper was at its worst and she knew she was being harsh with the foundlings when they howled. But she couldn't help it. Gin and brandy was the only thing that would put her to rights. In a way, if she spent the remaining two and sixpence at the Old Ship it would be as much for the foundlings' benefit as for hers. Her temper would be sweetened and once more she'd be as an angel to them. So surely it couldn't be sinful to aim to be kind?

She was thus fidgeting with her conscience and the two shillings and sixpence when Bostock poked his fierce head round the door and gave her a further two shillings for the poor.

"Bless my soul!" said Mrs. Bonney, patting Bostock's inky hand. "Another little Christian!"

"No I ain't," said Bostock sadly. "I'm a hypocrite, Mrs. Bonney."

"I don't care what domination you may be, Master B.," said Mrs. Bonney. "You're a real Christian to me."

# 13

SORLEY WAS ILL. Mrs. Alexander had noticed and mentioned to Mrs. Bunnion that the boy was sickly pale and showed signs of wasting away. Mrs. Bunnion had told her husband, but he had refused to believe it—as indeed he refused to believe anything of an unpleasant nature. Then he saw with his own eyes that the boy took no breakfast on the Wednesday and scarcely touched his lunch.

At once the headmaster plunged into an extreme of anxiety. Though a sensible and respected man whose scholarly accomplishments no one would have questioned, he was much given to extremes of alarm. They arose from the very weakness of his nature that caused him to ignore disagreeable matters. He knew this weakness and he despised and dreaded it; but he could not help it. He happened to be squeamish about omens of disaster. Thus, by the time something was actually forced on his notice, it had generally swollen to the gravest proportions.

In a matter of moments he had convinced himself that Sorley was dying. All the tangled troubles of the school and the duel sank away into idle dreams before the stark reality of Sorley's approaching death. He dispatched Ralph for Dr. Harris, even though he feared that the baronet's son was already beyond the physician's skill.

"I can make nothing of it," said Dr. Harris after he had examined the listless Sorley. "Everything seems in order—yet . . . ?" He prescribed one of Mr. Parrish's powders to stimulate Sorley's appetite and departed, leaving Sorley in nature's hands.

Dr. Bunnion saw him to his carriage and asked if he should inform Sir Walter of his son's condition. Dr. Harris, obsessed and distracted by his own strange tragedy, looked at the headmaster vaguely, at first nodding and then shaking his head. "Forgive me," he said, seeing the headmaster's bewildered look, "but I have troubles at home. As you must know, we have lost our youngest child."

Dr. Bunnion, who naturally took "lost" to mean the child had perished, expressed sympathy; but at the same time felt a pang of uneasiness. If the physician had been unable to save his own child, what hope was there for Sorley? It was exactly as he'd feared; Sorley was doomed.

He hurried back and administered Mr. Parrish's powder with his own hands, saying to the pale and haunted-looking boarder, "Never mind, boy—I will send for your father." He had no intention of sending for Sir Walter, as the thought of that great man terrified him; he had only meant to comfort the boy. Then he left the room, closing the door reverently behind him. When he returned, some two hours later, Sorley had gone.

The fat boy was running. At first he made for the town; but the sight of people frightened him and he turned towards the great green Downs. Sweat ran off him in streams and his cheeks shook and jumped till he felt they would tear away from his face.

He had been driven half mad with guilt. Mr. Brett had been following him everywhere, not letting him alone for an instant. Always the figure before him—always the hand on his shoulder, clutching tight. He did not know what it was he'd done, and that made it a thousand times worse. Had it been some particular crime he could have confessed it—as he'd done on the crust of the stolen pie; but it hadn't been the theft of the pie at all for the pursuit had gone relentlessly on. The very uncertainty of what it was about tormented him like a mortal disease. Sleep deserted him and food— his chief pleasure—tasted rancid in his mouth. What had he done? What had he done?

In anguish he dredged up every mean and petty act he'd ever committed, every paltry crime and dishonesty that crawled in the dark of his brain. He would confess them all. But there were so many! Every moment more came creeping out. Sins of the day, sins of the night, dark and unwholesome . . . How vile he was! To confess all was unnatural, impossible. Naked he trembled in his mind's eye, covered with misdeeds that scaled and erupted all over him like a leprosy of the soul.

His fat flesh seemed gummed to his clothing as the sweat congealed. He collapsed on the grass high up on the Downs and drifted into a terrified half sleep that was worse than no sleep at all.

He was not strong, clever nor brave, and in his deep self-examination he had wretchedly failed. The threat of his father coming to the school hung over him like a nameless sword. He dared not go back. If only—if only he'd had a friend! Even at home in Cuckfield he'd never had one. His mother scorned him for his absurd appearance, and his father despised him for his dread of all the great dogs and high horses that flashed yellow sneers at him wherever he went. The school had been a haven; Dr. Bunnion and his wife had been kind . . . so kind . . .

Extremity of distress drove Dr. Bunnion to extremities of discretion and he succeeded in concealing the loss of Sorley until after five o'clock when the day pupils had gone. There was nothing to be achieved by panic, he told himself over and over again.

Nor, on the other hand, was anything achieved by the lack of it. Despite immense searches—in the confines of the school and among the half-built houses nearby where pits and trenches gaped with horrid blackness, laced with jagged teeth of rubble—Sorley was not to be found.

"You must send for Sir Walter at once," Mrs. Bunnion urged; but the headmaster, clinging desperately to the notion of a schoolboy prank, kept shaking his head. "He is coming on Saturday, my dear. He has promised. What can it serve if he comes now? Why distress him prematurely?"

So the search continued with an energy and urgency that, had he known of it, would have moved the lonely, fat boy to tears. But then men, like teeth, are only valued when they've gone, and it takes a gap in the family, like a gap in the mouth, to sharpen the heart.

Major Alexander, seeing Dr. Bunnion's total absorption in the loss of Sorley, instantly feared his own concerns would go by the board and the as-good-as-promised dismissal of Mr. Brett would be forgotten in the general confusion. Thus Saturday's duel would become inevitable; honor demanding that he would have to face Ralph if his private condition was not met.

"Brett is to blame, sir," he muttered, whenever he had the opportunity. "He should have kept a closer eye on the boy. No good for the school. Negligent . . . negligent . . ."

Though the Major spoke sincerely, he was not to know that it had been the very closeness of Mr. Brett's eye that had done the damage. Nor was Mr. Brett himself aware of this as his only concern with Sorley had been to clutch on to him as a shield against any possible unpleasantness from Dr. Bunnion.

"Perhaps he's gone home?" Mr. Brett offered, timidly attempting to ease the headmaster's mind; but Dr. Bunnion only shook his massive head in which there was rooted the irrational dread that the angel of death had come for Sorley and had taken him, lock, stock and barrel.

After two and a half hours the search was halted for dinner, during which time the fat boarder's empty chair exercised a terrible fascination over all present and provoked in every breast fresh fears and thoughts that, often, had very little to do with Sorley but were concerned with the wider and more frightening business of living. Major Alexander thought of the sharp pains of violent death, and Mr. Brett thought of the sharper pains of severed love; while Tizzy Alexander found herself thinking of children left alone and remembering yet again the abandoned baby on the Downs.

Thus the disappearance of the fat boy took its place as yet another wave proceeding from the pebble that Bostock and Harris had cast into the sunshine calm of the previous Saturday afternoon.

And still Bostock and Harris went steadily on. Like a pair of cats intent on their prey, nothing deflected them as they moved through the long week towards its end . . . inadvertently drawing after them a tangle of threads that, minute by minute, became more and more hideously entwined.

They were on their way back from the poorhouse after having donated a further two shillings to the Foundlings. Mrs. Bonney had been there, but to Harris's interest she had been looking quite glazed and gave off strong whiffs of brandy. The extreme pleasure with which she'd fallen upon the new donation had suggested a great deal to Harris, and his hopes rose cautiously to the skies.

"Did you notice, Bosty?" he murmured to his friend. "She was hardly with us. It's my opinion that another five shillings will see her awash altogether. And then—"

But Bostock said nothing. Too many setbacks had lamed his spirit and injured his faith in his wonderful friend. And indeed it was possible that Harris had miscalculated. Mrs. Bonney was a large and seasoned lady and, though brought to the water's edge, so to speak, it might well have taken more than Harris estimated to get her afloat.

Although when Bostock and Harris called she had indeed been shining with spirits, her glaze wasn't so thick that she couldn't see through it. She still waited for the wet nurse's arrival before floating downstairs and across to the Old Ship. And she remained sufficiently in command of herself to be chilled by the sight of the stranger with the clubfoot. She was aware that brandy made her affectionate and talkative and was sensible enough to be uneasy of what she might say; so before she touched a single drop, she gave the inquiry agent an unmistakably hostile stare which said quite plainly that there would be trouble if he attempted to take advantage of her. Whereupon Mr. Raven—who shrank from all scenes not of his own making—rose uncomfortably to his feet and clumped outside.

Sorley stood up. The sun had gone from the sky. It was almost dark and new terrors seized him as the loneliness of the Downs crept upon him like a ghost. He felt hungry. Mr. Parrish's powder was doing its work. Even as he stood, staring longingly towards the little lights that had begun to wink and gleam about the bulky town like netted fireflies, his hunger increased until he began to feel quite faint and lightheaded.

Home! He would go home after all. He would catch a coach— he would go down to the Old Ship Inn. There was sure to be a coach going to Cuckfield. And if not, somebody would feed him. After all, they were all human . . . He could eat a horse. Maybe they'd give him one . . . an old one ready for the knackers? I *must* eat, thought Sorley desperately. I must eat or I'll die.

He began to walk—then to stumble—then to run. He leaped the little hillocks and sprouting tufts of nettles; he went like the wind and puffed the air as if to drive great argosies before him. He rushed upon the town in an ecstasy of hunger. Through street after street he pounded, towards the busy sounds of horses and harness and grumbling wheels and men's cheerful voices and the maddening, all-pervading smell of mutton and onions that the fat boy dreaded might be in his mind alone.

"Hungry—hungry!" he grunted. "Must eat—"

"And why not?" murmured a voice that seemed to come from the night itself. "And why not, my young friend?"

He stopped, falling almost to his knees. A figure was standing in his path; a sturdy, squarish man with a large, black clubfoot. "Sorley!" moaned the fat boy, by way of explanation for everything—his circumstance, his tragic appetite and his right to pity. "I'm Sorley—"

"*Sorley?*" The voice contained a thrill of excitement.

"Hungry—food—for the love of God—please!"

"What are you doing here?"

"Mr. Brett—always after me—no rest—don't know why—help me—help me—must eat!" The boy was almost incoherent with his unnatural hunger and exhaustion; lights danced in the air and among them were the stranger's eyes. He swayed as if he would fall.

"My poor, poor boy!" whispered the inquiry agent, putting out a hand to support him. "I never thought—I never guessed he would act so soon! Come—come!"

He led him through the front parlor of the inn and up the front stairs, thus avoiding the more popular back. Mr. Raven was trembling uncontrollably at this terrific turn his adversary had taken, and at the thought of how fate had directed his steps to intercept it.

Once in his room, he ordered a plate of mutton and onions for Sorley and laid him on the narrow bed to rest until his supper came. Then he sat and watched him while working away to accommodate him more precisely in the close-woven design.

At last there came a knock on the door to announce the mutton was outside.

"Here, my poor friend—eat," murmured the inquiry agent.

Once or twice, almost timidly, Mr. Raven asked him questions, skillfully innocent questions of nothing in particular—and of Mr. Brett. But it was of no use. Mr. Parrish's powder had so multiplied Sorley's appetite that the boy could do nothing but eat rapidly, fiercely and to the total exclusion of the world. So the inquiry agent held his peace till Sorley was done; then he asked him with great gentleness if he had anything to say, to confess. The word "confess" was very important to Mr. Raven as he'd always found its very softness tended to unlock the most obdurate lips.

Sorley stared at the stranger from the night who had taken him in and fed him. He peered about the little room and heard the faint jingle of harness from below. All seemed dreamlike, and most of all the stranger himself with the great black boot that put a period to his short left leg. Perhaps there was something nightmarish about him; but Sorley could not think ill of anyone who gave him food.

Confess . . . confess. The word ran round his brain like oil; then the dreadful memory of his flight to the Downs rose up within him and he remembered his multitude of guilt. It pressed against his chest like a banquet of sin. Confess . . . confess . . .

The stranger, sitting quietly by the window, outlined against the dark sky, seemed like a graven image. Such of his face as Sorley could make out, seemed gentle and innocent . . . so Sorley confessed.

At first he was hesitant, bleating only of little pilferings at home, then he grew bolder and gave up larger misdeeds. They seemed to keep each other company, his sins, for they ventured forth quite easily when together. They lost their shyness and came tumbling out. Sins of the day, sins of the night—everything, everything!

Sorley panted with excitement as he ridded himself of all his burdens. The sense of lightness and perfect freedom was intoxicating and, had he been able, he would have invented fresh crimes for the joy of confessing them. At last he came to the end. There was nothing more left. A great tiredness came over him and, at the same time, a vaguely nagging sense of shame. Uneasily he peered towards the still figure of the stranger in the window. To his relief and joy there was no revulsion on his face, no anger, even. There was only a small, sad smile. So Sorley sighed and went to sleep.

The inquiry agent stood up and crossed, very quietly, to the bed. He looked down on Sorley. This young human being had emptied out the contents of his darkest heart without restraint. Mr. Raven shook his head in bewilderment. Was it all so little—so trifling? Was there nothing blacker than this mere blush of gray? Was there no—et cetera?

For some minutes he stood, looking down; then he covered Sorley with a blanket and settled himself down in the uncomfortable chair to pass away the night. In a little while he too was asleep and their snores mingled harmoniously.

# 14

MRS. BUNNION HAD TAKEN it on herself to write to Sir Walter that his son had run away. She had seen that her husband's sense of discretion had so gone to his head that even when the boy failed to return that night, he still hoped to avoid a scandal by keeping the affair within the confines of the school. So, early next morning, she quietly sent a servant to hire a horse and ride over to Cuckfield with her letter. This done she settled back with the cool satisfaction of a wife who has done her husband's duty for him. She adopted an air of unshakable calm and in that way became a tower of strength to the headmaster.

"I don't know what I would have done without you," Dr. Bunnion was moved to say on more than one occasion. "If not for your support, my dear, the news of this tragedy would be all over the town by now—perhaps even in Cuckfield."

Mrs. Bunnion patted her husband's arm and smiled. If nothing else, the calamity of Sorley's disappearance had served to draw the headmaster and his wife closer together than they'd been in years.

But the effect on the other husband and wife in the school had not been so happy. Major Alexander had become very agitated and irritable, and the continuing sight of his wife calmly sewing while the world went up in flames, enraged him.

"And what the devil are you making now, madam?" he muttered, as Mrs. Alexander shook out the shapeless yardage of white linen she was stitching at. "A shroud for your husband on Saturday?"

*"Bitte?"* said Mrs. Alexander, firmly retreating into her native tongue.

Baffled, he turned away and stared at himself in the long glass that Mrs. Alexander used for studying the effects of her dressmaking. In it he saw a face seamed and shadowed with fear and distress. The mine he had so cunningly laid was in terrible danger of exploding beneath him. The cursed duel loomed ahead and there seemed to be nothing that would now avert it.

Honor—honor! What quagmires and pitfalls it led him into! Because of honor he could not withdraw his challenge unless Dr. Bunnion met his condition and got rid of Brett. Now the vanishing of Sorley had put paid to that. Brett, furtive and underhand as usual, had made himself indispensable. Because he'd been hanging about Sorley these last days, Dr. Bunnion clung to him as to a brother. Plainly he imagined that Brett had some special knowledge of Sorley's habits that would lead to his return. So long as the baronet's son was missing, there was no chance at all that Dr. Bunnion would dismiss Brett.

The man in the mirror was trapped, and bleakly the Major recognized himself as this luckless victim of honor. Even supposing there were other conditions he'd settle for—and, in his present state, the Major could have thought of hundreds—his own impetuous nature had rendered them out of the question. He had already written to his son. Tomorrow night, most likely, Adam would be presenting himself, loud with the news of Mr. Brett's dismissal—which would not have taken place—and louder still in his expectation of being employed in his stead. He knew there would be no keeping Adam quiet; not even the abbot at Basingstoke had been able to do that.

The Major bowed his head and Mrs. Alexander, taking advantage of the space, held up her stitching to the mirror to study the way it fell; thus when the Major looked again, it seemed for a moment there was a ghost over his shoulder—the ghost of himself.

"For God's sake, keep that thing out of my sight!"

"*Bitte?*" said Mrs. Alexander.

Brokenly the Major realized his only hope lay in pressing on vigorously with the duel until the headmaster came to his senses and cried a halt.

At the first opportunity, which was later that afternoon, he took Mr. Brett on one side and, reminding him earnestly of his duties as a second and a friend, instructed him to inform Ralph Bunnion's second that the duel would take place at eight o'clock on Saturday morning on the seashore opposite the Old Ship Inn. He chose this somewhat public place in the melancholy hope that Dr. Bunnion, when he heard of it, would be so alarmed at the prospect of the entire town's turning out to watch, that he'd accede to anything to prevent it. The more the Major thought about it, the more optimistic he became; he felt sure that in this way honor could at last be satisfied and he could live with himself on terms of mutual satisfaction and respect.

Soon after Mr. Brett had gone on his errand, which was about an hour before dinner, the Major seized the opportunity of remarking to Mrs. Bunnion that it seemed a shade negligent and even casual of Mr. Brett to leave the school when everyone was so concerned. Mrs. Bunnion nodded and said that she had every confidence that soon Mr. Brett would be leaving the school for good. Whereupon the Major reflected that honor, if pursued with sufficient industry, might still bring its own rewards.

Mr. Brett hastened through the town to get his unwelcome errand done with. A strong wind was blowing off the sea. The gulls were flying inland and it was possible to see a great distance over water. Plainly the fine weather was breaking up and Mr. Brett felt a sharp uneasiness for Sorley if he should be out in it. Indeed his concern for the fat boarder almost drove everything else out of his mind. Though he himself had suggested that the boy might have gone home, in his heart of hearts he didn't really believe it. He had once met Sorley's father.

The thought of fathers reminded him bitterly of the errand he was upon. So it was to be at eight o'clock on the seashore, with all the world looking on, that James Brett was to be revealed as the furtive scoundrel who had been acting for both the opposing parties in an affair of honor. No doubt there would be many who would imagine he had egged them on. Dully he wondered if Ralph Bunnion or the fiery Major would shoot him for his duplicity, or merely be content with kicking him out of the town. He thought of the bright contempt in Tizzy's eyes, and that was worst of all.

"O God!" he whispered. "Let the sun fall down from the sky before those eyes of hers turn as hard as stone! But what can I do? If there's a god in heaven—Zeus, Jupiter or Jehovah, I don't care which!—tell me what I can do?"

He paused, and the sea wind seemed to blow fiercely right through his head as if to clear it of rubbish and weeds for some new seeding . . .

He entered the back parlor of the Old Ship at about a quarter after seven. It was uncommonly noisy and he recognized the matron of the poorhouse exchanging loud unpleasantries with everyone present. In particular she seemed very angry with a man with a clubfoot whom Mr. Brett had seen several times before. She kept accusing him of trying to take advantage of her and he looked horribly embarrassed. The rest of the parlor, being temporarily spared, were clearly enjoying his plight and Mr. Brett felt quite sorry for him as he was no match for the lady in her high mood.

He wondered why the man didn't leave; but it turned out he was waiting for a plate of mutton, while the landlord, who wasn't hurrying himself, kept winking with pleasure at each of the lady's verbal thrusts. Then the man with the clubfoot happened to catch Mr. Brett's sympathetic eye. Inexplicably he paled and muttered, "Pity from you of all people!" Mr. Brett shrugged his shoulders and concluded that the man was weak in the head; then he saw Frederick sitting in a corner and nursing his mahogany pistol case. He began to make towards him.

"Two-faced!" shouted Mrs. Bonney suddenly; and Mr. Brett stopped in his tracks as the chance remark struck home.

"Not fit to be in company with decent Christians!"

The man with the clubfoot gave a sickly smile and attempted to murmur something to the landlord who grinned and nodded but did nothing more.

"There 'e goes!" warned Mrs. Bonney. "Watch 'im! Says one thing to your face and another be'ind your back! A Christian gentlewoman don't know where she is with 'im. Oo's drunk me brandy? Bleeding thieves! Oh, Gawd, where am I?" She sat down heavily and peered about her. "Where are you, Mr. Bonney? I can't wait 'ere all night!"

Then she became quiet, but continued to gaze about her with some anxiety—as if she was worried she was waiting in the wrong place.

Mr. Brett stared at her; an idea was stirring in his mind. An idea not unconnected with the coming duel and the expression on Mrs. Bonney's face.

Sorley was starving again. His extraordinary benefactor seemed to have been gone for hours. All day he'd remained in the little room, waited on hand and foot by the curious Mr. Raven. Whenever he'd asked to go out, Mr. Raven had warned and begged him to remain where he was as he was in great danger. Mr. Raven never said what this danger was, but his manner put the fear of God into Sorley. He had known all about the visit of Dr. Harris to the school, and when Sorley had told him about the powder he had been given, Mr. Raven had looked very troubled and grave.

This seemingly supernatural piece of knowledge had alarmed Sorley still further and he obeyed Mr. Raven willingly. Though people might have called him a fool, he certainly wasn't foolhardy; and anyway, Mr. Raven treated him so well. Sorley had never known such gentleness and even deference before. Towards afternoon he began to gain in confidence and quite put on airs. He found himself rather enjoying lording it in this little kingdom with its view of the sea. It tickled him no end to see Mr. Raven clump about on menial errands so readily.

That was why he began to feel alarmed and desperate when Mr. Raven was gone so long for his supper. It wasn't like him to keep Sorley waiting.

Sorley scowled and went to the door. The loud, angry voices he'd heard before had now subsided into a murmur. He opened the door. He remembered the way he'd come up. He wouldn't be so silly as to risk those stairs. He smiled cunningly—and went down the back stairs.

"*Sorley!*" roared Mr. Brett. "Come here, boy!"

# 15

DESPITE THE VIGOR of the gale that rattled the windows and buffeted the doors, the relief and joy on Sorley's return produced a burst of sunshine in almost every heart—Mrs. Bunnion and Major Alexander alone having slight reservations.

Though she would certainly never have wished Sorley ill, his untimely return presented Mrs. Bunnion with an unpleasant problem. Uncomfortably she watched her husband congratulating himself on the narrowness of his escape from an awkward and painful situation. Unfortunately, though he did not at present know it, he had not quite escaped. The servant who had taken Mrs. Bunnion's letter to Cuckfield had returned to her with the murmured news that Sir Walter Sorley would be arriving tomorrow. She sighed. She did not care to think how her husband would take what he would surely regard as an unwarranted going behind his back. Like all weak men—and Dr. Bunnion *was* a weak man—he was not apt to be indiscriminate in his anger and not pause to think.

Though considering the matter narrowly, Mrs. Bunnion was willing to admit that she *had* gone behind her husband's back; but it was only because, at the time, he'd been facing the wrong way. After all, he should have written the letter himself and not left it to her sense of fitness and duty. Supposing the worst had happened and Sorley had not been found; what then? Where would the headmaster have been if his wife had not written her timely letter? And now, because of the merest chance on Mr. Brett's part, Dr. Bunnion would never appreciate what a treasure he had in his wife. Anger would blind and destroy his judgment.

If only Mr. Brett had had the decency to wait another day, even . . . The more she thought of it, the harder she found it not to dislike the interfering way he'd come between husband and wife; much as she despised Major Alexander, she couldn't help agreeing with him that the sooner Mr. Brett went the better it would be for the school.

As for the Major himself, he was bitterly disappointed in the lack of resolution shown by Dr. Bunnion who now showered such esteem and gratitude on Mr. Brett that the Major felt quite sickened by it. Like all sly, furtive and underhand men, Mr. Brett had a gift for ingratiating himself at the expense of his betters.

"Very well done, Brett," said the Major warmly during the evening. "Delighted it should have been you who found him. Couldn't have happened to a nicer man!"

No matter what he thought privately of a man, the Major always believed in giving praise where it was due; or even where it wasn't, for that matter, so long as it served a worthwhile purpose.

The Major was fighting desperately to save his honor, and if at times he suspected that his conduct did not appear entirely straightforward, he knew it was because honor was the hardest of taskmasters and demanded the cruelest of sacrifices. As Mr. Brett was the particular sacrifice he still had in mind, he did not spare himself in his efforts to catch him unawares.

Mr. Brett smiled gratefully. He was in that state of mind when all the world was goodness and every man a friend. Had Tizzy Alexander come in his way that evening, he would undoubtedly have swept her up in his arms and put out the lights in her eyes and the fire in her lips with kisses that extinguished only to rekindle. But Dr. Bunnion kept plying him with port and congratulations till gradually he sank beneath both.

Then Dr. Bunnion went once more to reassure himself that Sorley's return was not a dream; after which he retired to bed, where Mrs. Bunnion overwhelmed him with such tenderness and affection as he had not known since the first nights of their marriage. "My dear," he murmured. "Life is so good . . ."

Mrs. Bunnion, veil-eyed in the dimness, smiled enigmatically, and trusted that her efforts would have kindled such a flame in her husband's heart that no unpleasantness to come would quite put it out.

Certainly it lasted through the Friday morning. Though the sky was full of dark clouds scudding towards London like black coaches stuffed with letters of dismay, Dr. Bunnion went his ways in a private sunshine. Not even the thought of the morrow's duel overcast it as much as it might have done. The vanishing of one shadow from his life went a long way towards dispelling the other; and he promised himself that he would apply himself vigorously to halting the whole insane venture—after lunch.

On his way down from Religious Instruction—which he'd left for the few remaining minutes in the charge of the most trustworthy pupil—he came upon Mrs. Bunnion who was unaccountably lingering in the hall. He twinkled his eyes with an almost mischievous knowingness. Life was so good . . .

Mrs. Bunnion smiled back with all the sweet mystery of a lovely woman whose powers are about to be put to the test. She had, at that very moment, seen Sir Walter Sorley dismount from his steaming horse and make for the door.

Fleetingly she wondered if she ought to prepare her husband for the blow that was about to fall; but before she could decide, it fell. The baronet had knocked, been admitted and called Dr. Bunnion a damned scoundrel who needed horse-whipping.

It had all been frighteningly sudden. Who had let him in was not very clear to Mrs. Bunnion. Perhaps she'd done so herself? He stood in the hall, panting and sweating slightly from the healthful exercise of his ride and demanding that a servant should attend to his horse. He did this with a directness that implied pretty strongly that if no one else was available, Mrs. Bunnion herself should oblige.

He was a strong, upright looking man, not so tall as Dr. Bunnion, but broader across the shoulders. His brow also was on the massive side, and his heavy, almost handsome, face had an expression of natural authority. He was, in truth, what he was always proud to call himself: an English country gentleman of the old school. It may not have been a very good school, but all such gentlemen seem to have gone to it.

"Bunnion! I trusted my boy to you—and now you've betrayed that trust! What the devil are you doing about finding him? Answer me, sir! Don't just stand there!"

Mrs. Bunnion looked to her husband in alarm. Although he was, as Sir Walter observed, standing, he was swaying slightly—as might some tall forest tree that has received the fatal stroke of the woodman's ax and totters before crashing to its ruin. A glazed and terrified look was in his eyes and he passed his hand across them.

Who had done this thing to him? Incredulously he stared at the baronet. How had the news reached him? Who had betrayed him? Some venomous servant, perhaps? Someone who ached for his destruction? Someone who hated him with a cold and implacable hatred?

All this Mrs. Bunnion read in her stricken husband's face; and her heart almost failed within her. How—*how* could she reveal to him that the vicious traitor was his gentle lover—the companion of his days and the comfort of his nights? That the hand that had written the fatal letter was the selfsame hand that had so sweetly caressed him? How could she strike him to the ground when he was in most need of support?

She could not do it. There comes a time when truth is no longer the shining sword of the angels, but rather the arrogant ax of the butcher. So Mrs. Bunnion trembled and held her tongue and prayed for a miracle to save her from discovery.

"My dear Sir Walter—my dear Sir Walter," moaned Dr. Bunnion, "I—I—" Then he was spared further explanation as the pupils came out to lunch. They roared and tumbled and thundered from their several classrooms and united in a single stream of immense force that flowed towards the wooden extension of the kitchen where the day boys ate.

"Papa!" shouted Sorley; and Sir Walter stared in angry bewilderment at his son.

"He—he was recovered yesterday," mouthed Mrs. Bunnion faintly above the din.

"Then why the devil wasn't I told?" The baronet's anger had taken another turn. Though no one could have questioned the depth of his feelings for his son, this sudden sight of him had thrown the baronet quite off course. During his great ride he had worked himself up into a state of pleasurable anticipation at the thought of browbeating the Bunnions. He was, at heart, a simple man and had simple pleasures. Now the unexpected sight of his son thwarted him and made him feel unnecessary and foolish.

Dr. Bunnion tried ineffectually to explain that it had all been a schoolboy prank . . . no cause for real alarm . . . in fact one of his own people had brought the boy back quite unharmed . . . everything all right now . . . and what pleasure and indeed an honor to have Sir Walter visit, even though, as it turned out, unnecessarily . . . would he care to stay to lunch?

"So you panicked, eh?" said Sir Walter, glancing contemptuously from husband to wife as the last of the boys eddied round him like a small ripple round an old pile. "Thought you'd lost your prize pig, eh?" Here he nodded to the portly Sorley who remained beside him. Suddenly he grinned. "Shouldn't wonder if you filled your breeches, eh, Bunnion?" He laughed, then observing that Mrs. Bunnion had gone very red, added, "Saving the lady's presence, eh? But I expect she knows what's what!"

Mrs. Bunnion curtsied feebly in acknowledgment. There was no doubt that Sir Walter, despite his rough exterior, was one of nature's gentlemen. In the farmyard anyone might have told him apart from the pigs; it was only in company that there might have been some difficulty.

He stayed to lunch. There was enough to eat as Mrs. Bunnion had no appetite. The discovery of her treachery had not yet been made and she had felt quite ill with apprehension. Once or twice her husband had muttered to her, "Who could have told him? Who could have been so vile?" but she'd shaken her head and had been unable to answer him; so Dr. Bunnion had lapsed into a state of listless despair in which the only consolation seemed to be that matters could get no worse.

But here he was mistaken. Sorley was stabbing him in the back. In order to ingratiate himself with his sport-loving father, the fat boy was telling him about the approaching duel. Despite all the headmaster's efforts, it had proved impossible to keep the affair from the pupils. Major Alexander had discovered that wagers were actually being laid among the boys; and he had been mortified to learn that the odds were heavily against him.

Now Dr. Bunnion was forced to sit and listen in helpless shame as Sorley acquainted his father with the affair in all its sordid details. He was amazed how much the boy had found out—and how his miserable brain had retained it all.

Dr. Bunnion knew he was done for. Nothing could survive such a scandal. The school would have to close. God knew how he would make a living. Not even an obscure curacy in some dingy parish would be open to him after this. The scoundrel who'd informed Sir Walter had done his work well. He was ruined beyond recall. But who—who could it have been?

He stared stonily down the table, and chanced to see Mr. Brett smiling to himself as if some private dream was about to come true. What dream? Then he saw Major Alexander frowning at Mr. Brett distastefully. Suddenly he recalled how the Major had warned him about Brett being furtive and sly.

"Brett!" he whispered to his wife. "It must have been Brett!"

"Oh no!" breathed Mrs. Bunnion. "I'm sure—he couldn't— oh, never! I can't believe it! Not Mr. Brett?"

"Brett!" repeated Dr. Bunnion bitterly; and Mrs. Bunnion,

feeling it hopeless to argue with her husband in his present mood, shrank back and let matters take what course they would.

In her heart she knew she was acting unwisely—that no scapegoat could or even should save her; but she was drowning and when a straw hove into view, she was inclined to clutch at it regardless of its propriety in holding her up.

"And where's that young stallion Ralph?" asked Sir Walter amiably. "A good lad even if he is only a schoolmaster's son."

Sir Walter did not mean to be offensive. He honestly liked Ralph and was well aware of the Bunnions' hopes concerning the lad and his daughter Maud. Frankly, he wasn't opposed to the match. Though a baronet, he was not a rich man and could spare little in the way of a dowry for his child. In fact, whoever took her off his hands would have to take her as she stood, with nothing but her shift and his noble name. If that was all right by the Bunnions, it was all right by him. Sir Walter, whatever faults some might have seen in him, was no snob. God in Heaven! He'd sent his son to be educated alongside a riffraff of tradesmen's brats! If his daughter married beneath her, he wouldn't break his heart; and the lad was well set up and would, most likely, breed clean.

Ralph was sent for and Major Alexander excused himself. Since the challenge it had not been thought discreet for the antagonists to sit at the same table. It would have created an embarrassment. This gentlemanly behavior had been proposed in the first place by Mr. Brett—to each of the principals separately—and had helped tremendously in keeping his own extraordinary situation from general discovery.

The baronet greeted Ralph kindly and hoped all would go well on the morrow. Had he known of the affair, he would have been pleased to act for Ralph himself as, being a gentleman, he had some knowledge of such sporting events. Then he went on to give Ralph sound advice on where and how to stand so as to present the smallest target. If the ground sloped, it was an advantage to be lower down as landscape offered a more confusing background than sky to one's opponent. Also, he said with a smirk, it was better to be hit above rather than below the waist.

"Ha—ha! We don't want you gelded, eh?" He stared round. "Saving the ladies' presence, eh, but I expect they know what's what!"

"*Bitte?*" said Mrs. Alexander.

"Bitter," agreed the baronet, grinning broadly. "Very! You've hit the nail on the head, ma'am! Bitter for his bride. Like a mare being served *by* a feedbag instead of *with* it!"

He laughed immoderately at this and only subsided when he saw the ladies were not joining him. "Mealymouthed lot," he grunted and returned to the business of powder and shot, but continued to look round hopefully whenever he had occasion to mention balls.

The duel was now inevitable. In spite of all Dr. Bunnion's intended efforts, the fatal event was to take place. The headmaster's spirits, briefly raised by the baronet's unexpected pleasure in the wretched business, had collapsed when the full enormity of it struck home. By tomorrow his only son would be either a murderer or a corpse. This was the reality.

"And yet it serves me right," he whispered to his wife in the privacy of their room which they were preparing to vacate for Sir Walter to sleep there that night. "It serves me right for being so meek and gentle. Believe me, my dear—oh, believe me—when the meek inherit the earth, I fear it's only six feet of it. O God, if only I'd listened to that well-meaning, honorable fellow Alexander and got rid of Brett days ago!"

"But—but is it too late?" murmured Mrs. Bunnion, an unworthy hope stirring.

"How can I dismiss him when everyone knows it was he who fetched Sorley back?"

"And—and if he stays there's really no hope of saving our son?"

"I couldn't approach Alexander again. The man has a fanatical sense of honor. He won't budge an inch . . . and then it will be all over the town . . . his wretched daughter . . . no!"

"Perhaps you could—put it to Mr. Brett? Surely he'll be human enough to listen? I'm sure he's a good man at heart. There is a kindness about him . . ."

Mrs. Bunnion was a deeply honest woman. She was doing her very best for Mr. Brett; and, short of owning up directly to her own unfortunate treachery which had not yet been discovered, it was hard to see how she could have acted more generously. Had anyone suggested she was deceiving herself she would have been rightly indignant.

"The man is a viper! He is furtive, underhand, sly! Never forget it was he who brought Sir Walter here! Never forget it was he who has ruined us!"

"Until he is proven guilty, my dear, I shall continue to believe in his innocence."

"You are too good and trusting, my love."

"Perhaps I am," said Mrs. Bunnion uneasily. "But I am a mother and have a mother's heart. I'm more inclined to forgive than you are, my dear. Whatever Mr. Brett may have done, I still believe in the goodness of his heart. If you choose to think the worst of him, I cannot prevent you. It is because you are a man and look at the world more sternly. To you, everything is either right or wrong. But to me there is no real wrong, only sadness and mistakes and things done for the best. All I can do is to try to soften you . . ."

"My love! If only I had such a heart as yours!"

"You have—you have!" whispered Mrs. Bunnion with a wistful smile. "I will go to Mr. Brett myself. I will plead with him for Ralph's sake. He will listen—I know he will listen."

"Be careful—be careful! I fear you are no match for him!"

A steely glint came into Mrs. Bunnion's eyes as if the very thought of Mr. Brett's being too much for her was insulting. "My dear," she said firmly, "even Mr. Brett has a mother; and it is as a mother I shall plead."

# 16

WHEN MRS. BUNNION LEFT her husband she had no fixed idea of what she should do. All she knew was that Mr. Brett must leave and somehow or other she must bring it about. She was prepared to go to any lengths to achieve this as she had by now fully persuaded herself that any sacrifice on her part was to save her son. Mothers throughout the ages had performed prodigies of heroism for their children, and she would not lag behind. Nature and custom sanctified her; and love lent a dignity to her intentions. She would exploit the full range of a woman's means to gain her ends, and no woman, so prepared, has ever failed. From the soft warmth of her mature charms to the icy force of her contempt, from anguished pleading to cataracts of reason, she would use all the weapons at her command. The prospect both excited and inspired her. She felt herself to be every-woman—all things to all men: lover and flail, mother and bride . . . Such was the concern of this woman for her child.

At no time at all was she ever directly moved by the consideration that, if she succeeded in getting rid of Mr. Brett, the blame for having written the unlucky letter might go with him as an uncustomed item in a general baggage of guilt.

While Mrs. Bunnion was thus troubled with thoughts of her child, the other mother in the distracted household was similarly occupied in this, the deepest business of nature. Mrs. Alexander, having at last finished her sewing, was attempting to guide the gentle torrent of Tizzy's black hair.

"Up, Ma. I like it up."

"A vooman's peauty is in her hair, *liebchen*. So vy make it look like a puddink? Ma knows best vat suits her child. Ah—like silk . . ."

And so it was; Tizzy couldn't help smiling in the glass.

"Look up, *liebchen*. Keep still . . ."

"Oh, Ma, I can't see a thing when you put them drops in my eyes."

"A vooman don't need to see, but only to be seen, *liebchen*. Ach—it makes your eyes look as deep and vide as the River Elbe at Hamburg."

"Really, Ma?"

"A man might fall in and lose his heart forever, *liebchen*. Ach! Vy vear your bodice so high? It vill choke you!"

"But, Ma—it won't be decent if it's any lower!"

"Decent? Decent? Vat's decent? *Liebchen*—I made your bodice; but Gott made vat's under it. So vy talk of decent? Ain't Gott's vork better than your ma's?"

"Oh, Ma!"

"So pink your cheeks! Like flowers!"

"I'm blushing, Ma."

"And how else should a man know ven he's kindled a fire? Gott is kind. Make a kiss with the lips, *liebchen*, and ve turn them into a rose."

"Not the lip rouge, Ma! It tastes like physic."

"And so it is, *liebchen*—but not for you! Now look in the glass and see how your ma knows best!"

Tizzy looked, but her eyes were misty from the belladonna, so she took her mother's word.

"And now, *liebchen*, it's time for the lesson; and may both of you learn."

As Tizzy rustled out of the room, Mrs. Alexander stared after her with tears in her worn blue eyes. They were tears of pride and hope, of memories and regrets. Then she turned back to the glass and gazed at her large, sad self. But her eyes were misty, too, and it seemed to her that the mirror still held Tizzy's reflection. "Gott is kind," she whispered. "Something sveet has come out of it all!"

Tizzy heard from somewhere the murmur of voices, then the loud laughter of Sir Walter Sorley. She bit her lip, tasted the lip rouge, made a face and attempted to hurry down the stairs. But cautiously. She could not see very well; and light made matters worse. Even a glimpse of the dull afternoon sky through a window provoked a rush of tears and turned the Academy into a house under the sea where stairs swam and walls were drifting and vague.

"Oh, Ma," she muttered as she stumbled and all but fell on the bottom stair, "a woman ought to be able to see where she's going!"

At last she found the classroom door. Will it be Ancient History all over again, she wondered with a quickly beating heart? Or will he see at last that there's something wonderful in the world today? She knocked.

"Come in."

Mr. Brett was standing. Little points of light seemed to be all over him. Tizzy could hardly bear to look at him, he was so splendid.

"Sit down," he said; and Tizzy thought she heard a tremble in his voice. She lowered her eyes and found her place in the front row where Bostock sat during the day.

The seat and desk were on the small side and her yellow muslin gown overflowed and streamed to the floor like a pool of dappled sunshine. She tried to arrange it becomingly, and knocked down a book. Mr. Brett moved to pick it up but Tizzy inadvertently forestalled him. She looked up, and his face glimmered large. She wasn't sure whether he was looking at the book or at her. She blushed and didn't know whether to bless or blame her ma. But either way there was something about Mr. Brett that had never been before . . . and, for a moment, Tizzy really fancied he was drowning in her eyes.

"Where were we?" he said, resuming his place. Tizzy's heart

misgave her; was it really to be Ancient History again? She braved the light and turned her eyes to where she dimly saw his face.

Just then a corner of the sun broke through the thick sky and sent a dusty golden shaft down into the room. The flies danced like tiny jewels and Mr. Brett dissolved in glory.

"Did I tell you of how Jupiter loved Io?" asked Mr. Brett softly.

"And turned her into a cow," said Tizzy, thinking of many marriages and with tears welling helplessly out of her eyes.

"Did I tell you how Leander loved Hero?" murmured Mr. Brett.

"And was drowned for it," said Tizzy, smiling sadly at Mr. Brett through her salty veils.

"Did I tell you how Antony loved Cleopatra?" whispered Mr. Brett, moved powerfully by Tizzy's emotion.

"And killed himself," nodded Tizzy. "And then she did, too, and they were buried in the same grave."

She tried to make out how Mr. Brett was looking—if he was smiling or serious. But she could not be sure; her drugged eyes had changed him into something dreamlike. His wig seemed turned to a silver helmet with a nodding plume, and the face beneath seemed carved out of the softer parts of sleep.

"Did I tell you of how Romeo loved Juliet?" breathed Mr. Brett.

"And did himself in like Antony before him?" whispered Tizzy. "Poor Juliet, poor Cleopatra, poor Hero! Is love always such a widowing thing?"

"Did I ever tell you," sighed Mr. Brett, now fathoms deep in Tizzy's eyes, "that your eyes are like mysterious, twilit pools, and your lips are a pair of kissing cherries?"

"No," whispered Tizzy. "You never did."

Then his face grew perfectly enormous and she stood up to meet him and hoped he could see better than she, the nearest way to a kiss.

For an instant she wondered if the lip rouge would put him off; but it didn't—not in the smallest degree. Oh, Ma, thought Tizzy, through a gap in her joy, you was right after all!

"I've loved you for so long, Tizzy Alexander!" murmured Mr. Brett, drawing breath for another kiss. "With all my heart and strength!"

"Then why didn't you say so before?" said Tizzy. "Because I've loved you, James Brett, for at least as long as you've loved me!"

Then they kissed again while the classroom flies danced in the shaft of sunlight and the world spun idly like a child's toy, a million miles below.

*"Mr. Brett!"* The voice came like a sword between them, and severed, they fell apart.

"For God's sake, Mr. Brett—and you, girl—have you no shame?"

Mrs. Bunnion stood in the doorway, her eyes flashing and her fine bosom heaving. "And in a classroom, too!" Fully prepared to sacrifice herself, she had come gently to Mr. Brett, thus her sense of outrage at the scene that confronted her was quite sincere. She was appalled. "I don't blame you, sir. I blame that—that Miss Alexander. First my own son—now you. But you must understand, sir, I—we cannot have it! Not in the school. You must leave, Mr. Brett. At once!"

In every way Mrs. Bunnion was an exceptional woman. Her

sense of justice never deserted her. She could still defend Mr. Brett's character even though, at the same time, she was able to urge his departure for the good of all. No one could have said that the thought of private advantage had moved her in the least.

"And as for you, miss," she said, staring bitterly at the tearful and disheveled Tizzy, "I shall spare your mother and father what I have just seen. Not for your sake, but for theirs; they have suffered enough on your account. I trust that you, Mr. Brett, will also be discreet. Please go quietly. Leave a note; say you have been called away on family affairs. I will support you, sir—and also respect you for sparing us all any further unpleasantness."

Here the quality of Mrs. Bunnion's virtue proved more than its own reward. If Mr. Brett did oblige and leave as discreetly as she proposed, then her own somewhat high-handed dismissal of him would never come out. Being human, she couldn't help feeling a distinct sense of satisfaction at the convenience of it all.

"Go?" said Mr. Brett palely. "Now? After I've—?" He glanced at Tizzy as if the sight of her loveliness was more eloquent than further words. Mrs. Bunnion shrugged her shoulders.

"No!" said Mr. Brett suddenly—to everyone's surprise and his own most of all. "I *will not* go. Let your husband dismiss me himself. And let him find a better reason—if he can—than my love for Miss Alexander. You may shout the house down, Mrs. Bunnion— *but I won't go!*"

Mrs. Bunnion stared at him. There was amazement and even terror in her eyes. A fly buzzed and settled on her pale cheek; but she seemed not to notice. Then, as if awakening from a sudden dream, she turned abruptly and left the room. She had been shaken to the depths of her soul. Mr. Brett's refusal had been like an earthquake in which the firm pavements of her existence had cracked and yawned asunder. Mr. Brett's departure had been her only hope of avoiding the discovery of her damning letter. Now that hope was gone. Her marriage, her life itself would be laid in ruins.

She did not return to her husband. She was not able to face him. Instead she went to their bedroom and looked about it with inexpressible anguish. She remained thus for several minutes till at last, dully surmising that life must go on to its bitter end, she set to work gathering together such intimate belongings as she and her husband would require for the night. Since they were obliged to make way for Sir Walter, they had fixed on sleeping in Mr. Brett's room and Mr. Brett was to be with the boarders. Mechanically she plucked at the pillows and opened and closed drawers without understanding or even seeing anything that lay within. How—how had it all come about, she wondered miserably. In a few days—no more—in a few days her brisk and comfortable world had been plunged into despair. How had it happened?

Bostock and Harris, in a mood of tense exultation, were on their way to the poorhouse. Bostock was wearing his oversized blue coat and was carrying an embroidered quilt from his mother's bed as the evening was windy and Adelaide might catch cold.

Yes; at last the time had come. On their last visit to the poorhouse Mrs. Bonney had been in so advanced a state of oblivion that Harris was convinced a mortal frame could withstand no more. Success this evening was certain; Bostock's waning confidence in his friend was quite restored, and Harris pointed out that when it was all over they would still be eight shillings in pocket.

"We could lay two shillings on Ralph Bunnion for tomorrow," said Harris shrewdly. Bostock nodded. Like everyone else, he was on the school hero's side. The heavy odds on Ralph Bunnion's victory in the coming duel was really no reflection on Major Alexander's ability. It was the expression of a general hope rather than a certainty that the best man would win. Had the Major been the deadliest marksman in all the land and Ralph the poorest, such hearts as Bostock's would still have wagered all on Ralph's success; and so, too, would Harris's—though a shade less impulsively.

"Here we are, Bosty, old friend," whispered Harris as they reached the scratched and battered door of the poorhouse. "If Mrs. Bonney ain't in the Old Ship, she'll be in her bed as brandied as a butterball."

The two friends entered the gloomy house in which the unmoving air was ripe with the smell of babies, gin and fish. They crept upstairs to the long, low room where the foundlings bubbled and slept.

"There she is, Bosty," breathed Harris triumphantly. "Down at the end."

Bostock advanced, his coat unbuttoned and ready, and flapping gently like the grubby plumage of some ancient bird. He had actually laid the embroidered quilt across the bleak little cot when . . .

"Gor' bless me! If it ain't me two little Christians come to cheer me Friday night!"

Mrs. Bonney, veiled in brandy, had risen from her bed. She stood in the doorway, blinking and swaying, but unmistakably awake. Her frame must have been more than mortal. Six shillings' worth of spirits had done little more than dent her.

"All donations is welcome," she said and stumbled down the room with hands outstretched. Even in her present state, charity was uppermost in her mind.

Harris, whiter than Bostock had ever seen him, fumbled in his pocket.

"Here, ma'am!" he croaked. "For—for the poor!" In a panic he gave her the whole eight shillings.

"If only there was more like you," said Mrs. Bonney moistly, "this ol' world would be a 'appier place. You'll go straight to 'eaven, Master H. You'll gallop right through them gates in a coach and four! And so will you, Master B.—right alongside of 'im!"

She had seen the embroidered quilt. She took it up and pressed it to her glassy cheek. "All donations is very welcome . . ."

"My ma took three years to make that quilt," muttered Bostock in the street outside, overcome by his misfortune. "What'll she say when she finds it's gone?"

"What's a quilt compared to a live baby?" said Harris with the weary bitterness of one plagued by trifles. "We ain't got Adelaide, either."

"Three years," said Bostock, hurt by Harris's attitude. "And it don't take as long as that to make a baby, Harris."

Harris, a shade unnerved by the unusual workings of Bostock's mind, looked at him almost with respect. "Bosty, old friend, we can't give up now. We're so near to it. As sure as my name's Harris, eight shillings' worth of brandy'll pickle her cold. Tomorrow morning, Bosty. Early. We'll try for the last time. I promise, it'll be the last time."

Bostock thought, then shrugged his shoulders and sighed. After all, they were friends. "We'll miss the duel, Harris."

"We've got nothing left to bet with, Bosty. And anyway, my sister comes first. Poor little Adelaide! She must be wondering what's happening."

Mrs. Bonney, divided between taking the beautiful quilt up to grace her bed and going straight to the Old Ship, decided on the latter. She fancied she'd heard Mr. Bonney come in so it wasn't as though she was leaving the foundlings untended.

"Evening all," she said to the little parlor at large, and sat herself down to a night of very good cheer indeed. God alone knew she'd earned it. Nobody but a lady in a similar walk of life could know the trials of charitable work. With high satisfaction she observed, out of the dim corner of her eye, that the brute with the clubfoot had taken himself off into the shadows to avoid her. Good riddance! He crowded her; and once in her cups, Mrs. Bonney liked plenty of room to swim.

Mr. Raven went up to his lonely little room. There was an ache in his heart as he stared at the forlorn and empty bed. He remembered Sorley and the warmth of confession. He remembered looking after him . . . until that devil Brett had taken him away. He, Raven, had been powerless to prevent it. His strength was all in his mind; he would have been no match for a man like Brett—and his wry foot put pursuit out of the question. But tomorrow he would hurl his thunderbolt!

He went over to the table and took the papers out of his pocket. He spread them out and studied the affair of Adelaide Harris. The ever-increasing complexity had now extended over two large sheets, and the inquiry agent had some difficulty in remembering how they fitted together.

The whole conspiracy was represented by a tremendous number

of lines, crossing, joining, dividing and intertwining to form the pattern of a spider's web. At various points of intersection, names were trapped like helpless flies: Dr. Harris and his wife, the Bonneys, the Bunnions, the entire Hemp household, Morgan the nurse, the gypsy baby, Adelaide Harris, Frederick and the landlord of the Old Ship who always said "good riddance!" whenever Mr. Raven left the parlor. But right in the middle of this diabolical plan, like the terrible spider he was, crouched the inquiry agent's great adversary, Mr. Brett.

Long, long he brooded over it, careless of the fading light. He moved his finger from place to place, murmuring, "Et cetera, et cetera," and drawing ever nearer to the vital spot that, once cut, would destroy the whole unclean thing and reduce it to a heap of meaningless threads; then, with nothing to support it, the deadly creature in the middle would come crashing to the ground to be squashed under the inquiry agent's avenging boot.

At last his finger halted. He had found the vital spot. "The thunderbolt," he whispered. "Who would have thought it?"

# 17

NIGHT, DARK AND IMPENETRABLE, seemed to collapse over Dr. Bunnion's Academy rather than fall in the usual way. Moon, stars and all the high paraphernalia of the heavens were utterly obscured by banking clouds that the wind had gathered in a great black rubbish dump above the town. Here and there uneasy candles gleamed out of windows as curtains were briefly drawn aside.

Major Alexander looked out often. His son Adam had not yet arrived and the Major clung to the frail hope that he would not come. Sometimes he fancied he glimpsed a striding figure in the dark; then he'd hold his breath and wait for a loud knock on the front door. But no such knock came and the Major concluded what he'd seen had been a trick of the shadows or a ghost.

Ghosts were much on his mind; twice he'd imagined he'd seen his own in the long glass in his room. He was not a superstitious man, but he felt there was something ominous in the air—an invisible iron curtain that was slowly shutting him off from the world of men. He felt horribly lonely and would have been glad even of his wife's company; but she was with Tizzy so he cursed her German soul. He should have married an Englishwoman; she at least would have understood him—and understood an Englishman's honor.

He paused in his pacing and gazed into the glass. He tended to examine his figure rather than his countenance, for it was an unfortunate disability of his that he was unable to look even himself in the face. In his military days, this natural drawback had given him an unlucky reputation for shiftiness, which no efforts on his part had been able to dispel.

Well—he was out of that now. He had kept himself to himself and no one but his wife thought ill of him . . . damn her German soul! If he died tomorrow he would die as the man of honor he really believed he was. It paid to be secretive and not to demean oneself with friends. It was decent strangers who took their hats off when a man of honor's coffin went by. Filthy friends would be all too apt to say, "There goes shifty Alexander. Caught at last!"

Inadvertently, his eyes met his reflection's. "Liar!" he whispered. "Liar, liar!" He had seen a face gray with dread, and lips that seemed to writhe over the terrible words, "I don't want to die! Please, Ralph, don't shoot me!"

The striding figure the Major had glimpsed in the night had not been a ghost. It had been Mr. Brett. The thought of sleep had been intolerable and the dark grandeur of the night had drawn him out. He looked up and was surprised how low the sky seemed; even the trees were not so tall as they'd seemed yesterday. Mr. Brett felt twice his old height, but very light and strong in his movements.

She loved him! Tizzy—enchanting Tizzy—Tizzy of the marvelous eyes and lips as sweet as ripe cherries—he could taste them yet! Glorious, blushing Tizzy in the sunshine of her dress whose bodice, try as it might, could scarcely subdue the pride of her breasts. She loved him and had said so. What more had the world to offer? Crowns, glory, fortune and even fine weather were but trumpery items, sops thrown to the millions to make up for not having Tizzy.

At last everything stood in due proportion. First things had finally come first, and Mr. Brett laughed aloud as he recalled his defiance of the awesome Mrs. Bunnion. Love was his general and Tizzy his flag; so inspired he could conquer the world.

But now he'd best go inside. It was coming on to rain and there was no sense in falling to a chill before he was more than love's lip servant. As he entered the school a vague memory of having been told something about the night's arrangements crossed his mind. He paused, frowning slightly in an effort to pin it down. No; he couldn't remember. Perhaps it would come to him later.

He went upstairs, light as a feather, and humming, slipped into his remote little room. Mrs. Bunnion was in his bed. She stared at him in terror.

"Oh my God!" said Mr. Brett; and remembered what he'd been told. He was to sleep with the boarders as the Bunnions were to have his room for the night.

"What do you want with me?" whispered Mrs. Bunnion. Her husband, after futile attempts to share the narrow bed, had gone down to the sofa in his study and left her alone.

"I—I forgot," said Mr. Brett uneasily, staring at the magnificent Mrs. Bunnion whose hair streamed across his pillow like the banners of yesterday.

"I thought—I hoped—I prayed you had come to—to say you had changed your mind."

"I'm sorry, Mrs. Bunnion."

Uncomfortably he saw her eyes were puffy with crying. Surely she couldn't be so concerned about the school? Or was it Ralph and the duel that was so distressing her?

"If it's Ralph—" he began; but she shook her head and her tears came on again. "Oh, Jack, Jack!" she sobbed.

"James," said Mr. Brett firmly. "It's James. But I don't suppose it matters now."

Mrs. Bunnion looked at him and managed a faint smile. She really was rather lovely—in a time-worn way, and Mr. Brett caught himself wondering by what declension she'd come to be the headmaster's wife.

"You must love Miss Alexander very much," said Mrs. Bunnion gently. He nodded. "She is a—a pretty girl."

*Pretty?* Mr. Brett was amazed at such a belittlement.

"All young girls are pretty, James. Even I was; once." Here she gave so sad a smile that Mr. Brett forgave her for undervaluing Tizzy.

"And so you are now, Mrs. Bunnion," he said gallantly. "Your husband is a very lucky man."

"My husband?" she whispered. "Lucky?" And then it seemed to the startled Mr. Brett that the gates of her heart burst open to a final flood of despair. At first she covered her face with her hands as if still seeking some privacy in her grief. Then she was forced to abandon this as she could not draw the great, broken breaths she needed to sustain herself, nor easily expel them in the long stairways of sobs down which she seemed to be tumbling and falling with frightened jerks of her shoulders and head.

Quite consumed with pity, Mr. Brett watched her, not daring to move or speak. Then Mrs. Bunnion told him why she wanted him to go. She confessed what she had done and how she had hoped his departure would carry away her guilt. She told him that she was no longer young, and that all her life meant was to be with her husband; that there was nothing else for her, and that to lose him would be to lose everything. Such love as there was between them was not like the love of the young. It was no longer a blaze from which many another brand might be lighted; it was a gentle, forlorn glow in a large and empty night. There were no other brands anymore; there was but the husband and the wife.

Mr. Brett remained silent. He did not know what to say. This scene of human fear and misery dazed him. Stupidly and irrelevantly all he could think of was that he would have to go to bed without his night things as it was impossible to start looking for them now. "Good night, ma'am," he mumbled, and left the room.

He went down to his classroom, the place of his triumph. He sat at his desk and stared over the shadowy seats that were unnaturally quiet. There were not even any ghosts to comfort him; he was utterly alone. What did his victory mean? Someone else's defeat. He frowned and rubbed his eyes. Must success always bankrupt another? Can nothing be won without inflicting despair elsewhere? Was this the only way of the world?

What if he agreed to take the blame for the letter? For a moment this seemed possible; then he shook his head. Dr. Bunnion would dismiss him in such a rage that Mrs. Bunnion would be compelled to confess.

He opened his desk and fumbled for paper and ink. There were two letters for him to write. One was to Dr. Bunnion, explaining that he'd been called away on family business; the other was to Mrs. Bunnion, begging her to look after Tizzy and tell her he loved her dearly and would send for her when he could. He did not really believe that such a time would ever come, but the essential gentleness of his nature made him offer this forlorn hope.

When the letters were written, he left one in his classroom and, after listening for sounds of Mrs. Bunnion and concluding she was asleep, pushed the other under her door. Then he returned to his classroom to gather such books as he kept there, and settled himself down as best he could and waited for the dawn. He would have to leave his clothes where they were, in the wardrobe in his room; but this extra sacrifice seemed to lend an added nobility to his renunciation.

Upstairs, Mrs. Bunnion had not been asleep. She had seen the letter appear under the door and had lain quite still for several minutes, not daring to take it up. Another crushing disappointment was more than she could endure. At length she could bear it no longer.

She read Mr. Brett's letter three times over, as if unable to believe it. Then she lay back on the bed and stared at the ceiling. "Thank God!" she whispered. "Thank God!"

Beside her the night-candle flickered wildly till, with a sudden splutter and gulp, it went out. But Mrs. Bunnion, the letter still clutched in her hand, was already fast asleep.

# 18

SATURDAY'S WAS A MORNING made for farewells. The rain was falling heavily, as if to hurry everyone on their way and then wash out all trace of them. From time to time there were vague flashes of lightning and distant, impatient grumbles of thunder. Major Alexander, who'd woken early, looked out on it all with melancholy satisfaction; at least such weather made the world not so hard to leave.

It completed also Mr. Brett's misery as he slipped out of the school and hastened through the teeming air. He was going to the Old Ship to get a coach to anywhere; and if he caught a chill on the way and died of it, so much the better—so much the better for all. He knew he was being noble, but he got no pleasure from it—and wondered if anybody ever did.

It was scarcely five o'clock and the town was still asleep, so he was surprised to see someone trudging towards him. At first he took the other to be an early washerwoman, then he saw it was a young man in a monk's gown. The young man was quite extraordinarily wet and his pleasant, innocent face with its crown of fair hair stuck out of his gown like a washed stick of celery poking out of a sack.

Taking him for a member of some charitable order, Mr. Brett wished him good morning and offered him a shilling. The young man thanked him, took it and squinted up at the glum sky.

"What we need, sir," he said surprisingly, "is a God for today."

"Indeed," agreed Mr. Brett; "if He'd stop it raining for us."

But this did not seem to be what the young man had in mind, for he frowned at Mr. Brett and continued on his soaking way. Mr. Brett smiled after him. There was something he'd rather liked about the wayward monk. There was something about his features that had reminded him of someone . . .

At last Adam Alexander, who'd had to walk a good part of the way from Southwark, drew near to Dr. Bunnion's Academy. The shilling he'd just been given would have been much more useful ten miles back; but then he was used to God being out of date and too late.

At last, there it was standing before him; his new home!

He approached the front door and was about to knock when it opened and his father appeared before him.

"Can't explain now!" muttered the Major, seizing his son's cassock with nervous violence. "But come round the back, lad. And for pity's sake, hold your tongue!"

Mrs. Alexander, whose ears were quite as sharp as her husband's, for the first time in many a long year had occasion to bless the arrival of her son. As soon as she was certain the Major was somewhere at the back of the house and occupied in silencing Adam, she left her room and went in search of Mr. Brett. He was not with the boarders so she suspected him of mooning in his classroom. But he wasn't there, either. She was about to leave when she noticed a letter on his desk. It was addressed to Dr. Bunnion, but trifles like that did not bother her. Where her daughter's happiness was concerned, she was capable of great feats of dishonesty. To be frank, Mrs. Alexander, deep down, was not a particularly honest woman; it was perhaps this quality that had first attracted the Major.

She opened the letter and read it. She scowled. She had half expected Mr. Brett to run away. In her experience all men—except her husband—tried to escape once they felt themselves to be entrapped. She sighed and shook her head. Not for nothing had she lived so long with the ex-Major of Engineers. She had made preparations. And anyway, she thought to herself as she hurried to her daughter's room, if he got away from Tizzy, he'd be caught by somebody else, and maybe by somebody not half so good as her Tizzy. So she was really doing him a kindness . . .

"Qvick, *liebchen*! Up! Dress! Ve'll cetch him yet! Hurry—hurry! Everything is mended and packed. Qvickly! Gott forbid you should be left behind and have to marry such a man as did your ma. He loves you—and you love him! It's natural! Vat more do you vant?"

When Mr. Brett reached the Old Ship there was no one about but a pair of horse boys playing dice under a projecting roof in the inn-yard. After some moments during which he became absently interested in their game, he asked them when the first coach would be pulling out.

"Where to, mister?"

"Anywhere . . . anywhere at all."

The boys grinned at each other. "Coach going to Southampton at about eight."

Southampton! A misty vision of ships sailing to forgetfulness filled his aching mind. "Is there anywhere I can wait till it leaves?"

"Not for an hour or more, mister."

"May I shelter here?"

"Suit yourself, mister; only don't get in the way of the dice."

Mr. Brett nodded and knelt down beside the players. After a little while he became fascinated enough to ask if he might join them. After all, what had he to lose, except money? The boys stared at one another, then grinned again.

"Suit yourself, mister—so long as you play fair. Remember, we ain't much more'n children."

So he began to play, at first winning and then losing so steadily that he began to wonder if there was more skill in the game than he'd thought. Sometimes he suspected one or the other of them to be cheating; but he couldn't see how it might be done. Besides, they always looked so childishly surprised when they won . . .

"Gawd 'elp us!" said one of them suddenly. "There's someone

comin'! Thanks for the game, mister!" They grabbed their winnings and, with the speed of stable rats, scuttled away and vanished.

"So you have so much money you can throw it away, Herr Prett? Tizzy, *liebchen*, it's a gambler you are marrying!"

Then Mrs. Alexander broke down and cried her eyes out while her daughter was in her lover's arms. "And—and don't forget to give him the veddink shirt, *liebchen*! I finished it only yesterday, Herr Prett!"


At about half past six a loud rattle of thunder awoke Mr. Raven. "Yes!" he whispered to the grim bulge of his boot under the blanket; then he stared through the filthy window to the thick sky. "And the day is made for it!" He left his bed and fetched in his other boot which he always left outside the door, though more as a gesture than anything else as it hadn't been cleaned for days. Then he dressed and clumped downstairs for his morning brandy and water.

The landlord was not yet about, so the inquiry agent wandered to a window that looked out onto the yard. He stiffened with excitement. He had seen them! Brett and the woman he had good reason to know as Maggie Hemp. Brett was smiling, laughing; he seemed possessed by a spirit of ruthless gaiety. He caught sight of the inquiry agent's terrible face. He waved and grinned and put his arm about the female, Hemp.

A nerve twitched and jumped inside Mr. Raven's huge boot so that it beat on the floor like an enormous wounded bird. The inquiry agent had seen baggage. The malevolent pair were on the point of escaping! *This* he had not expected!

"When does the first coach leave?" His voice trembled as he asked the potboy who came in, surly and slow, to take his order.

"Eight o'clock. Southampton."

"Eight o'clock!" The inquiry agent groaned harshly. Even the ordinary affairs of daily life seemed to work in favor of his adversary. At eight o'clock other matters would be afoot; matters of life and death and et cetera. What was he to do? For the first time he cursed the burden of his boot. He could not move quickly enough.

He closed his eyes. He must not panic. Panic was the death of thought. He looked out of the window again. He caught his breath. The baggage was plainly the female's. Brett had none. Mr. Raven smiled; he understood. Brett was not going.

Once more Brett's eyes met his—and this time the inquiry agent returned his cheerful wave with an ironic inclination of the head. How nearly the Devil had succeeded in panicking him, thought Mr. Raven grimly; but he was not to be bluffed. "Laugh and grin to your heart's content," he murmured. "But I know what I know, et cetera . . . ."

Faintly he heard the potboy muttering to someone at the back, "Brandy an' water at this time in the morning! I tell you, he ain't human!"

But Mr. Raven was human; all too much so. In some men, being human was a sign of strength; in Mr. Raven it was definitely a weakness. He smiled at the potboy when his drink came and wondered whether it was too late to enmesh him in the web. He attempted to call up in his mind the immensely complicated tangle of intrigue to see if there was a space for the insolent potboy. But it was hopeless. No mortal mind could envisage that plan in all its tortured detail.

At length he could bear it no longer and the continuing sight of

Brett and his paramour aggravated him terribly. He swallowed his drink and stumbled back to his room. With trembling hands he spread out the grotesque plan again and stared, for the last time, on the tangled lives and murderous plots that comprised the Adelaide affair. His finger moved from place to place, but it was in vain. The design was complete and the potboy would have to go to the Devil on his own.

Carefully he folded up the plan and thrust it into his boot. "You'll keep the secret, eh?" he chuckled. Again the nerve twitched and his boot shuddered. The plan, perhaps meaningless to a casual observer, fairly screamed to Selwyn Raven that a murderer was moving along one of the spidery lines towards a certain intersection where there waited the man to be murdered. But the inquiry agent had the measure of it all. Brett's bluff had failed and all the monsters were doomed. The time had come for Mr. Raven to launch his thunderbolt. He struck his boot to stop it trembling and then clumped unobtrusively out of the Old Ship and made his way towards the house of Dr. Harris, where he had not been asked to stay to lunch . . .

# 19

UTTERLY WORN OUT by her night of grieving, Mrs. Bunnion still slept. Mr. Brett's letter had fallen from her hand to the floor. No one else in the house knew that he had gone.

In the kitchen extension, tragically unaware that the duel need now no longer take place, Major Alexander was making his peace with his son and apologizing for having brought him so far for nothing. There was no vacancy in the school; there was only approaching tragedy. Still, he was glad to see Adam for what might well turn out to be the last time. He felt that, of all people, Adam was the only one who understood him. They were very close.

"Come, Father," murmured Adam, embarrassed by the Major's display of emotion, "it's not over yet. There's still hope."

But the Major shook his head. All his elaborate schemes had misfired, and he was morbidly convinced his pistol would do the same. "Whatever anyone says of me, son—*afterwards*, you'll know I acted honorably. To know that will be a great comfort to me. It's all been only for your sister's good name. Perhaps I was wrong to put family honor so high, but such is my nature. And I feel yours is the same, son. I know, if you had been here, you would have done the same."

"I'll stand by you, Father!" said Adam impulsively. The Major thanked him, but couldn't help being a shade disappointed that Adam hadn't offered to stand *for* him, instead. The more he thought of it, the more this failure of Adam's depressed him and a slight cloud overcast their relationship. A lifetime's habits of suspicion were not so easily cast off, and the hapless Major found himself wondering if his son's eagerness to remain by his side was not prompted by the hope of another, more frightful vacancy?

The Major was a complex man, and suffered in a complicated fashion. But his opponent, Ralph Bunnion, was simple and did not suffer at all. Almost dressed, he was sharing a bottle of claret with the jovial Sir Walter Sorley. Indeed, his greatest concern seemed to be for what waistcoat he should wear for the occasion; thus he was in the tradition of all those heroes who love to show death more re-spect than life. The love-lies-bleeding he rejected on account of its unfortunate associations, while the love-in-idleness was stained. At last he fixed on an elegant creation of love-in-the-mist that Dolly Packer had done for him in the old days.

"Bleeding, idleness and mist," he murmured in an unusual mood of poetry. "It's like life, isn't it, Sir Walter. First the wound, then the resting, and then the uncertainty of it all."

Sir Walter sniggered and said it reminded him of marriage. Ralph frowned and put his waistcoat on. It was probably his most beautiful garment, having, in addition to the purple flowers, sev-eral finely woven silver plumes twining down towards the edges.

"Pretty, isn't it," said Ralph proudly. Sir Walter grinned.

"And witty, too," he chuckled. "Old man's beard, I fancy. Couldn't you keep up with her, lad?" Here Sir Walter fairly choked with laughter, spraying claret all over himself in a fine red rain.

"It's traveler's joy!" said Ralph indignantly.

"You know best," said Sir Walter, wiping himself dry. "You and the—the lady. Oh lord! Couldn't keep up with her! D'you get it? Must tell Maud and Lady Sorley!"

While the two men were thus preparing themselves for the fatal occasion, Dr. Harris, who was to attend one or the other of them, adjusted his wig and scowled at himself in the glass. The idiotic duel. As if he didn't have enough to worry about! Nearly a week had gone by and there was still no news of Adelaide. Though he had by no means given up hope, he was beginning to feel that gnawing dread at his heart that he always experienced when he knew a patient was dying. Bitterly he felt that Captain Bostock had failed in his duty; he had done nothing and had been content to leave everything to Mr. Raven. Dr. Harris's confidence in the inquiry agent had waned. He had already paid him twenty-five pounds and all the fellow seemed to do was to drink brandy at the Old Ship. And all the while the weird gypsy infant lay in Adelaide's cot.

Slowly the doctor packed his bag with such instruments as he might need. Privately he was convinced the two fools would miss each other; but he was cautious enough to go prepared for the worst. Bandages, forceps, scalpel, brandy . . . was that all? He fastened the bag and, observing the heavy rain, took out a cape. He would rather have waited for the wet nurse, but she didn't come till after eight. Still, Morgan would stay with Mrs. Harris and not leave her alone with the baby. There was no doubt his wife's hatred of the infant had become more acute in the last days. He went down the stairs. Damn Selwyn Raven! He would give the man until midday and then the gypsy baby would go straight to the Bonneys at the poorhouse. He had had enough!

He opened the front door. Bandages . . . forceps . . . scalpel . . . brandy . . . From force of habit he told off the contents of his bag to make sure nothing had been forgotten. He paused, shook his head; then, half humorously, he shrugged his shoulders and went back for a prayer book. "Just in case," he murmured. "Just in case . . ." Then he went out to his carriage which was already waiting.

Some two minutes after the doctor had gone, his front door opened again and his son emerged, carrying an old piece of blanket. He looked rapidly up and down the street, blessed the teeming rain that was keeping the townsfolk within doors, and hastened away to collect his friend. The change in the weather *must* mean a change in their luck, thought Harris; and he felt in his bones that all was set for success at last.

Unhappily no such optimism attended Major Alexander as he and his son set out from the school at approximately the same time as Harris met Bostock at the other end of the town.

"What about mother?" asked Adam. "Oughtn't you—we to say good-bye?"

"Much she cares," said the Major bitterly. "Damn her German soul!"

"And Mr. Brett?"

"We'll meet him there."

Ralph Bunnion, on the other hand, having no cause to be bitter with anyone save Tizzy Alexander, lingered to say good-bye to his father. Mrs. Bunnion, it turned out, was still asleep and the headmaster didn't want to waken her as he couldn't bear the thought of her distress at the parting scene. With tears in his eyes he wished Ralph well, and then lapsed into the apathy of despair from which he'd been disturbed. Thus it was a good ten minutes after the Major and Adam had gone that Ralph and Sir Walter Sorley set off confidently for the fatal meeting.

"What about your seconds, lad? Your friend with the pistols and that fellow Brett?"

"We'll meet them there."

The rain lashed down on the town with unabated fury and Frederick, walking briskly to the dueling ground with the mahogany pistol case under his arm, prayed that the powder would not get wet. He stopped and took off his cloak and wrapped the case inside it. It would be horrible if one of the weapons failed to discharge and someone was killed by the other. It would make him feel like a murderer. In a few moments he was wet to the skin; but at least the pistols were keeping dry and his friend would have a fair chance. He consulted the little silver and enamel watch that someone had left in one of his father's coaches. The time was twenty-five minutes to eight; so he quickened his pace.

The inquiry agent had arrived at Dr. Harris's house. He had been terribly hampered by his boot which was full of rainwater and so was twice its ordinary weight. Furiously he banged on the door—and kept banging till a frightened maid appeared.

"Your master!" shouted Mr. Raven. "Where is he?"

"Gone out."

"Already—already? Fetch your mistress. Quick—quick!"

Mrs. Harris, hearing the commotion, had already come down. The inquiry agent stared at her savagely. Her name was on the paper in his boot, caught in that frightful web. She was a guilty woman. All women were guilty.

"Give me the baby," he snarled. "I know everything, Mrs. Harris. *Everything!*" She stared at him, at first not taking in what he'd said. Then a look of joyous amazement lit up her face. Adelaide! He had found her!

"Thank God!" she wept. "Morgan—quick! Fetch the baby!"

Perhaps had her mind not been so distraught with anguish and had she not loathed the gypsy child so much; perhaps had her husband been at home, even, Mrs. Harris would not have been so hasty.

"Wait!" she pleaded. "Wait while I dress, Mr. Raven!"

"No!" he answered harshly. "There is no time. A life is at stake."

At twenty minutes to eight, with the gypsy brat stoutly wrapped and held in his powerful arms, the inquiry agent left the Harrises' house and stumbled through the rain.

So—at last, they were all out in the open and going their several ways: the duelists, the inquiry agent, the gypsy brat—and Bostock and Harris. The selfsame rain came down and soaked them all as if in a universal dismay at the prospect before them.

The baby had begun to cry, but all the world was crying and Mr. Raven told it so. Then it peered up at him through slitted eyes, and the inquiry agent shuddered at the inquity in them.

It was possible that at some time during this final journey he had doubts as to the course he'd determined on; but doubts at all stages of an enterprise are part of the human condition. He was right to doubt; he was neither a beast of the field nor a god. He was a man—and men may be wrong. A little higher than the beasts, a little lower than the gods, man is ever a double loser. For a pinch of divine understanding he has sacrificed his instincts; therefore a man should always have his doubts, and et cetera . . .

Fiercely Mr. Raven cast his mind back to the affair's beginning (while struggling to shield his burden from the rain); the bizarre appearance of the strange baby in Adelaide Harris's cot. Only an explanation as bizarre as the event itself would answer it. And there was no doubt Mr. Raven had provided such an explanation.

But then never knowing for certain how an event has begun, a man can only guide his understanding along the path of his own experience. Thus some men look up to the great sky and see God; others see but the blind and empty stars. Either way a man is condemned to build his tower on the shifting sands of doubt. The best he can do is to struggle as high as he can, then make his divine leap. Mr. Selwyn Raven nodded his head, and struggled on to make his divine leap.

Two other voyagers in the rain, namely Bostock and Harris, had reached the poorhouse. They were very wet and somber. Bostock's mood was partly due to the distress in his home at the loss of the quilt, while Harris's was because he felt he had reached the end of a road. All his courage, all his ingenuity—and all his money—had been staked on this last endeavor. If he failed and Mrs. Bonney wasn't dead drunk, then Adelaide was lost forever. So also would be the esteem of Bostock; and, in a strange way, Bostock counted for more than anything. Bostock was his friend and had always looked up to him. Where would Bostock be without him—and where would he be without Bostock?

Harris scowled. "This is it, Bosty old friend."

Bostock stared at him, and Harris fancied there was a coolness in Bostock's eyes. "This is it, Harris."

The friends shook hands and pushed open the poorhouse door.

Within, the air was curiously strong. The ordinary smell of fish, gin and babies was overlaid with something sharper and yet richer. It was not in itself the smell of brandy, and yet there was brandy in it. It resembled more than anything a heavy cake that had been burnt. It was very powerful on the stairs and grew more so as the friends mounted. At last they reached the room where the foundlings lay; and the smell was tremendous. Bostock and Harris stopped in the doorway. They trembled.

There was a chair at the far end of the room, and in the chair, wrapped in Mrs. Bostock's quilt, sat Mrs. Bonney. Her eyes were partly open but they gave no glimmer of recognition. The smell, now in great waves, was coming from her. As Harris had promised, the last eight shillings had done it. She was as brandied as a butterball and she stank like a vat.

"Christians," she mumbled weirdly as Bostock eased off his mother's quilt. "Darlin' Christians at it again . . ."


Mr. Raven had made his divine leap. With a last muttered, "And et cetera," he had laid the gypsy brat outside the house of the Hemps. *The Hemps?* Yes, the Hemps. Where else should the thunderbolt fall?

He had rapped on the door, then hobbled into concealment to a flash of lightning and a clap of thunder. Then he waited, his reputation at stake. If he was right—and still he was human enough to fear he might be wrong—then this one dramatic stroke would bring everything tumbling out of the cupboards of Hell and into the light of day. He fumbled in his boot for one last glimpse of his plan. He drew it out. It was sodden with rainwater. Every last name and line had run into a filthy pool of ink. No human being could ever have made any sense of it. It was lost forever. Mr. Raven cursed; then he grew still.

The door had opened. The elder Miss Morgan looked out, looked down. She screamed. Mr. Raven sighed with relief—and smiled.

The elder Miss Morgan crossed herself. Though she'd never clapped eyes on it before, she recognized the weird infant from her sister's account. The worst had happened; the fateful spell she'd given away had come home to roost. She screamed again. (Mr. Raven hugged himself.) The foul goblins had laid the changeling at *her* door. If it entered in the house, then all the hellish mystery of Celtic ghosts would be let loose to break the plates and drive everyone storybook mad.

Careless of the rain she knelt down, snatched up the wrinkled fiend and rushed away down the street. She would leave it where it could do nobody any harm.

Mr. Raven watched after her and wondered where she might be going. He would like to have followed, but he dared not. He was waiting for the murder. Very soon now, he had good reason to believe, Ralph Tomcat Bunnion would attempt to assassinate Indian or, rather, Gypsy Hemp. He hoped to God he would be able to prevent it.


Harris kissed his infant sister. He was sincerely glad to see her again; there were times when he never thought he would. Bostock looked on, deeply moved. Then the friends, watched by the insensible Mrs. Bonney, crept out of the room with the quilted Adelaide in her brother's arms.

"Harris," whispered Bostock as they were on the stairs. "What about the other one? What do we do about the baby at your house?"

Harris looked at him. He had entirely overlooked the other baby. He couldn't think of everything; but he wasn't going to admit it to his friend. Bostock's faith in him was in the melting pot.

To confess to an oversight now would be to crack the mold and let Bostock's faith trickle away altogether.

"First things first, Bosty," he whispered, and continued down the stairs.

"Harris!" gasped Bostock as they opened the poorhouse door. "Oh, Harris, you're a genius!"

On the step before them lay the alien baby where the terrified elder Miss Morgan had deposited it a moment before.

"Christians," sighed Mrs. Bonney, as Bostock and Harris laid the gypsy child in the empty place. "Bleedin' Christians comin' and goin' like pink mice . . ."

# 20

THE RAIN WAS BEGINNING to give over. A stout sea wind was bundling the clouds towards London and a distant glitter of sunlight had appeared on the gray sea's horizon. Mrs. Harris, her daughters and Morgan the nurse, unable to bear the suspense of waiting indoors, had been scouring the nearby streets for some sign of the triumphant inquiry agent with Adelaide in his arms. Caped and hooded, they leaned and turned into every gust of wind with their garments whipping like broken wings. Mrs. Bostock, looking out from her window, saw them and begged them to come inside—at least until the worst of the wind had dropped. At first

Mrs. Harris wouldn't hear of it; but when Mrs. Bostock declared that a physician's wife should know better than to court a severe chill, she saw the sense of it and, with her soaking family, accepted Mrs. Bostock's kind invitation.

It was while she was waiting there, sitting in Mrs. Bostock's parlor and drinking hot soup, that Bostock and Harris returned Adelaide to her proper place. The emptiness of the house—which had been left in the care of the kitchen maid who would never come out of the kitchen since Morgan had warned her about goblins—and the consequent ease with which the friends accomplished their task, prompted Bostock to declare once again that Harris was a genius.

"I suppose I must be," said Harris dreamily. "But, Bosty, old friend, it don't make me feel any different from you."

Bostock stared at him disbelievingly. Was it possible that Harris really felt as vague and puzzled by the world as he did?

"I get the bellyache just like you do, Bosty; and the rain makes me just as wet."

Bostock smiled and shook his head. Harris was having him on. "It's the way you think, Harris; high, like an eagle."

"It seems quite ordinary to me, Bosty. Honestly it does."

Suddenly there came a knocking on the front door that put a period to all meditation. "It's the wet nurse! Quick—the window! Help me down, Bosty!"


At five minutes after eight o'clock, Harris, strolling into his home from nowhere in particular, was greeted with the most astonishing news. Adelaide had been restored! She was back—his little sister had come home!

He was overjoyed. His real warmth of affection and great delight surprised even his sisters who were glad enough to answer his many eager questions as to how the miracle had come about. The wet nurse had been admitted by the kitchen maid, he was told, and taken up to the nursery. She had come out almost directly saying the baby had been changed and looked amazingly like a poorhouse brat of her acquaintance. At first the maid had pooh-pooh'd her, thinking her to be in gin and not able to tell one baby from another as she saw so many. Then the wet nurse had lost her temper and flounced off so the maid had conquered her fear of goblins and gone in to see for herself. "Adelaide!" she'd shrieked—and then tumbled straight out into the street shouting, "She's back! Miss Adelaide's come back!"

Actually it turned out that Mrs. Harris, drinking soup at the Bostocks', had heard the cry some moments before anyone else, but had not dared to say so for fear she should be imagining it; but then Morgan heard it, and then everyone did. They all rushed out in a terrific commotion—the Bostocks included—and sure enough, Adelaide was back!

All this was told to the openmouthed Harris at such a rate and with so many interruptions—for the sisters disagreed on details— that the poor boy was quite bewildered and kept staring round the room in helpless amazement.

"But who—" he managed at length, "but who did it?"

"Why that inquiry agent, of course. Mr. Raven. It was all his doing."

Harris nodded. Mr. Raven, of course . . .

"And Ma says you're to go down to the Old Ship and ask him to lunch. Go on, hurry up now. Adelaide'll still be here when you come back!"

---

But the inquiry agent was not at the Old Ship. Nor was he still outside the house of the Hemps. Eight o'clock had been and gone and no pistol shot had broken the morning air. The murder had been forestalled—as he'd hoped it would—so Mr. Raven had clumped off to Dr. Bunnion's school to pick up the traces of his archenemy Brett. But when he got there he found the school in an end-of-term confusion with no one willing or able to help him. Not a soul seemed to know where the devil Brett had gone. Mrs. Bunnion, who had at last woken up, had gone flying out in a hopeless attempt to prevent the unnecessary duel, and the headmaster himself was doing what he could to conceal his agonized fear that Ralph, now two hours gone, was bleeding to death from Major Alexander's merciless bullet.

"Of course you know," said Mr. Raven, irritated by his casual reception, "that Brett was at the bottom of everything?"

Distractedly Dr. Bunnion nodded. "That is exactly what I keep telling my wife, sir."

"You villain, James Brett! You terrible, crafty, shocking villain! If Ma had only known, she'd never have let me fall in love with you!"

The time was shortly after nine o'clock; the place was the warmly dancing interior of the Southampton coach, now well on its way. The speaker was Tizzy Alexander, and *her* place was in the arms of her Mr. Brett. The cause of her censure was that Mr. Brett had just confessed to her his unusual part in the duel—and just what he'd done about it.

She was looking at him with great severity, and frowning with all her might. But the corners of her mouth, do what she would, kept tugging and twitching, and her shoulders were beginning to heave and shake. "James Brett," she began; but could say no more. Laughter engulfed her, helpless laughter that came bubbling up and exploding in her eyes. She rocked with it, and the coach rocked with her; and then Mr. Brett joined in and the tears ran from their eyes in shining streams while an outside passenger nearly overturned himself in an effort to see what was going on.

"But what else could I do?" gasped Mr. Brett. "What else *could* I do?"

Tizzy only shook her head and, when she was able to speak, all she could say was, "Do you think they're still there?" and then she was off again.

At a quarter to ten o'clock, Major Alexander and his son, Adam, cold, wet and ankles awash—for the tide was coming in—retreated from the seashore. "As I suspected," said the Major with grim satisfaction. "The fellow's a coward and won't face me!"

High on the Downs, near where Adelaide had been found, Ralph Bunnion and his party waited perhaps five minutes longer on account of not wanting to disappoint Sir Walter and to outface a small number of spectators who were beginning to jeer.

"I knew the swine was craven when I first clapped eyes on him," grunted the baronet. "All those damned military fellows are the same. Shoot your eyes out with a cannon, but not with a pistol. You have to get too close for that!"

Then they too left the dueling ground, with Frederick half glad his pistols had not been put to the test.

"And what the devil happened to that fellow Brett?" said Sir Walter as they walked along.

"And where was Mr. Brett?" said Adam Alexander to his father as they neared the school.

But it was not until the thwarted duelists met that they discovered Mr. Brett's duplicity.

"I told him that it was to be on the beach by the Old Ship," said Major Alexander furiously.

"He told me it was to be on the Downs," said Ralph Bunnion, equally annoyed.

"The man's a damned scoundrel!" said Major Alexander. "He has insulted an affair of honor!"

Mr. Brett had taken the only advantage possible in being second to both parties. He had arranged for them to meet some three miles apart.

"I warned you!" snarled the Major, glaring at Dr. Bunnion's knees. "I told you the man was furtive, underhand and sly!" Then he went off with Ralph and Sir Walter to Ralph's room where, heedless of gathering parents, the three men of blood and honor drowned their furious disappointment and humiliation in bottomless tankards of claret as red as their unshed blood.

Mrs. Alexander shrugged her ample shoulders and muttered something in her native tongue. Then her eye fell upon her firebrand son, Adam. She smiled sadly at him, and he, touched, laid his arm around her shoulders. Who knows, she wondered to herself in German, perhaps, in time, I might make something of him?

Mrs. Bunnion alone still had a good word to say for Mr. Brett; and whenever her husband recalled his treachery, she always defended him warmly and declared she couldn't believe it of him.

Then Dr. Bunnion would smile and say, "What a heart you have, my love. Generous to a fault."

As for the headmaster himself, now that all his fears had proved groundless and nothing disagreeable had happened, he was more convinced than ever that nothing was to be gained by facing an unpleasantness but a nasty shock.

Mr. Raven did not have lunch with the Harrises on that memorable Saturday, even though they pressed him to stay. He had sworn that he'd not break bread with them even if they begged him on bended knees. He did not want their lunch and he scorned their hospitality. He suspected he'd have been asked to eat in the kitchen. Besides, his work there was done. The return of Adelaide he took as a matter of course; he was pleased but not surprised. According to his plan, it had been bound to happen —and happen it had. The greater triumph was what had not happened. There had been no murder. This was indeed a feather in his cap; but alas, not the one he really wanted. Brett had escaped him. At the last minute he must have decided that the inquiry agent had come too close. So Mr. Raven was on his way to Southampton to track his adversary down. He and his boot would be the eternal pursuers, and Mr. Brett and his paramour would be the eternal pursued. To the ends of the earth he'd follow them, with his terrible tap-thump . . . tap-thump . . .

Had Tizzy and James been aware of this, they might indeed have been chilled; but the ship that took them to the crisp New World was too full of dreaming to let so lame a nightmare in; and the raven had no wings.

———

But back to that tremendous Saturday once more. One small mishap marred the general rejoicing in the homes of the Bostocks and the Harrises. Mrs. Bostock, returning unexpectedly from the Harrises, came upon her son attempting to dry out her quilt that had vanished mysteriously on the previous day and now appeared even more mysteriously. Despite Bostock's protests, she snatched it from him, and then she recoiled. It stank of fish, gin, babies and a very powerful odor that seemed to be compounded of brandy and burned cake. And so, Mrs. Bostock remembered, did the infant Adelaide.

She communicated this interesting fact to her husband who at once passed it on to Dr. Harris. The two fathers stared at each other. They grew very pale. Then, basely acting on suspicion alone, Captain Bostock thrashed Bostock with an old belaying pin he kept as a souvenir; but Dr. Harris, who was a more cultured man altogether, smote Harris with a volume of Harvey's *Circulation of the Blood*.

"Violence," said Harris the younger bitterly. "Personal violence. And only on suspicion, too."

"My pa said it was natural justice," mumbled Bostock, whose thicker feelings had not been so outraged.

"Justice? What's that? There ain't no such thing as justice, Bosty. It—it's just the calling card of brute force. Mark my words, Bosty; beware of the man who says he's just. He's the one who's out to get you if he can!"

Deeply impressed, Bostock nodded, and the two friends thereupon made a solemn pact to steer clear of justice in all its forms.

———

At the school Adam Alexander filled the vacancy created by the elopement of Mr. Brett, so Major Alexander's schemes at last bore a somewhat mottled fruit. Whether there was any justice in this or not is neither here nor there. It happened in accordance with the way of the world which is chiefly concerned with convenience